California Betrayal

Katelyn Marie Peterson

2021, Amore Moon Publishing – TWB Press

California Betrayal

Edited by Terry Wright

Cover Art by Terry Wright

ISBN: 978-1-944045-84-5

To my grandmother, Chiara Hannon, my favorite cheerleader.

California Betrayal is a fast-paced and moving story about family, betrayal, and the power of forgiveness.

Susan Breen, author of the Maggie Dove mystery series

Chapter 1
Thursday

On the fifth floor of a swank New York City apartment, Shay Collins felt as if she were waking up from a dream and walking into a nightmare. She stared at her luggage by the door and worried over what fresh hell she would stumble into this weekend.

"Are you sure about this?" Caroline asked from behind her.

"I don't want to miss my brother's wedding."

"You left California for a reason, to get away from your mother. You're asking for trouble."

"I'm only going to be there a few days."

Caroline looked at Shay with concerned eyes. They had been friends since they were kids. Caroline knew her better than anyone and knew a trip back home, even for a weekend, would not end well for her.

"Okay." Caroline sighed. "Call me when you get there."

"I'll be back Monday." She looped the strap of her black leather purse over her shoulder. "Oh, and please make sure Chloe gets to bed by 8:00 tonight."

"She'll be fine, but aren't you pissed that Sherry wants an adult-only wedding?"

"At least Chloe doesn't have to miss pre-school."

"True."

Shay picked up her suitcase and duffle and lugged them downstairs to a waiting cab. Once seated, she wondered if she had made the right decision. Caroline was right about her; she'd left an overbearing and manipulative mother who'd always managed to make her feel like a massive failure. No reason to think Janine had changed. Her most recent bone to pick was the fact that Shay was a 29-year-old divorcee, another failure. She also dreaded seeing her ex-husband again. Matt Blanco lived one town over from her parents' house in Renwick. She had divorced that alcoholic prick a year ago, before moving to New York with Chloe and Caroline. Like Shay, Caroline was also going through a bad breakup and needed a fresh start.

Both women were nervous to start over in such a big, complex city, but after a few months, they had figured it out, for the most part. Caroline found a job at a local clothing store where she became the assistant manager, and Shay landed a great job as a copy editor for a major publisher. She loved her job for many reasons, but among them was the fact that she got to work from home two days a week.

As she was thinking about her past and all the ways this trip could go wrong, the cab stopped in front of JFK airport. She decided to enjoy the journey and push her worries aside until she reached California.

Once she settled in on the plane, she received a text from Caroline: *Have a safe flight and call me if you need me to come out there and straighten out your mom.*

Shay smiled. Though she knew Caroline was joking, it was nice to know she had a friend she could always count on.

As Shay sat there waiting for the plane to take off, she thought about the day she and Caroline met.

It was her first day of kindergarten. Shay's father had just walked her into Mrs. Peterman's class, and like any child reaching a new milestone, Shay was nervous. All she wanted to do was follow her father out the door and never leave his side, but instead, she found a quiet corner in the back of the room and watched her classmates play with one another.

As Shay sat there, feeling the urge to cry and run home, a chubby little girl with curly brown hair and red-framed glasses walked up to her. She was carrying a coloring book and a box of crayons. "Hi, I'm Caroline. Do you want to color with me?" She pointed to the Disney princess on the cover.

"Okay." Cinderella was Shay's favorite princess.

That simple exchange was the beginning of a long-lasting friendship between Shay Collins and Caroline Fisher.

Her pleasant flashback was interrupted by a flight attendant's voice on the intercom. *"Folks, please stow your belongings in the overhead or under the seat in front of you."*

Once everyone was seated, the cabin door closed, and the jet was pushed back from the gate. While taxiing to the runway, the flight attendant demonstrated the safety equipment and pointed out the emergency exits. "Enjoy your flight to California."

Shay took a deep breath. *Here goes nothing.*

Chapter 2

The flight was calming. Shay forgot her troubles by taking in the beautiful view outside her window, the tapestries of farms and fields, the webbing of roads and rivers, and the ribbons of mountain ranges below. It also helped that the flight attendant came by selling drinks; a Vodka-7up really mellowed her out. However, once the plane landed, the butterflies resurfaced and the mellow mood faded.

When she entered the terminal, she saw Steve holding a sign: *Welcome home Shay.*

She gave her brother a big hug. It felt so good to see him again, but she was surprised his soon-to-be wife was absent.

"You have no idea how much I've missed you...but where's my future sister-in-law?" Shay looked around the concourse.

"Sherry would have loved to be here, but a couple of her girlfriends decided to surprise her and take her out for lunch. She'll probably be back by the time we get to Mom and Dad's."

"I can't wait to catch up with her."

"She'll be excited to see you too."

After a stop at baggage claim, Steve grabbed her bags and led her to the car.

Though Shay genuinely liked Sherry, a part of her was happy she wasn't there. It had been so long since Shay had seen her brother, she felt long overdue for some bonding time with him.

She and Steve had always been close, though Janine would often compare Shay's failures to Steve's successes. He was a straight-A student, an all-star athlete, from high school to college, and a dependable volunteer for multiple charities. And to top all that off, Steve had stellar good looks: thick wavy-blond hair, with not a strand out of place, piercing blue eyes, and a flawless complexion.

Her brother was perfect in every way.

As far as she was concerned, he was the best brother any sister could ask for.

"So..." Steve tossed her bags on the back seat. "I was thinking we could get something to eat before going to the house. Sound good?"

"Sounds great."

He started the car. "Penny's Pancake House? Are you good with that?"

"Breakfast this time of day?"

"They have a lunch and dinner menu, as well."

"Super. After that flight, I could eat a horse."

While they were on their way to the diner, Shay's phone chimed in a text message. She dug it out of her purse and opened the app. *Tony? Duh?*

Tony: *Hey, sexy. When are you coming back?*

Shay: *Monday.*

Tony: *Will I see you then?*

Shay: *Maybe later in the week. I'll want to spend some make-up time with Chloe first.*

Tony: *No worries. See you soon.*

Tony Perillo was a co-worker and friend with benefits. He was tall, with green eyes and jet-black hair, and he was built like the models she'd seen on the covers of magazines, six-pack abs and biceps that made her feel safe when he held her. Problem was, sometimes he seemed more enamored with his own body than hers.

As she placed the phone back in her purse, Steve parked the car, and then they headed inside the diner. As soon as they took their seats and placed their order, she immediately brought up his impending nuptials. "I still can't believe my baby brother is getting married. You must be so excited."

"Sherry's amazing. I can't believe she said yes."

"I'm happy for you. Sherry's a great girl."

"After Corrine left, I didn't think I'd ever find love again."

"Her loss—" Before she could get another word out, their food came. She took a bite of her bacon burger. "Did the guys throw you a bachelor party?"

Steve smiled. "We went to Vegas last week."

"Vegas, huh? I don't see any tattoos or piercings, so I assume you didn't get too wild." Shay laughed.

"Ha, very funny. Jason was in charge, so he kept us in line."

Jason Kent was her close friend growing up and the guy she secretly loved all through high school. After her divorce they'd reconnected, but when she moved to New York, their relationship faded from constant phone calls to short texts here and there. Eventually their hectic lives interfered, and they'd stopped communicating altogether. Such was the nature of long-distance relationships. So when Steve told her that Jason was going to be his best man, she knew all those feelings she once had would come rushing back the minute she laid eyes on him.

Steve snapped his fingers. "Hello? You still there?"

"I was thinking about Chloe," she lied. "I've never been away from her this long."

"She'll be okay." Steve smirked. "Aren't you excited to see Jason again?"

"Maybe."

"I knew it. That's why you're here. Why else would you risk facing Mom?"

"I'm here for you, Steve, to see you get married and wish you better luck than I had with my marriage."

"Yeah. You're a good sister."

That stung a little because she knew differently. When the going got tough here at home, she'd run away to New York, as far as she could get from California. This weekend she'd face the music for that desperate decision.

Chapter 3

Once the car pulled into the driveway, Shay stepped out and grabbed her bags from the back seat. Then, with her luggage in hand, she stared at her childhood home with a reminiscing gaze. It was a beautiful white raised-ranch with blue shutters and a spacious backyard, perfect for running around and playing silly games with Steve. Aside from the constant squabbles with her mother, she really did love growing up there.

Steve stepped up beside her. "You ready?"

"Not really," she said with a nervous laugh.

He put a comforting hand on her shoulder. "It'll be fine." Then he stepped forward, prepared to be her buffer, like always.

Whenever she and Janine got into an

argument, he would step in and cover Shay's back. One time, after a particularly nasty spat, she was so angry, she ran out of the house. "I'm leaving and never coming back." Steve chased after her and led her to a place in the woods. There was a nice stream and rocks of all sizes, some perfect for skipping across the water. Steve called it his *thinking spot* and offered to share it with her. It was a peaceful, though temporary, escape from her mother.

As they started walking toward the door, Steve turned around and smiled. "Just breathe. It might not be that bad."

Then, just as he was about to turn the knob, the door swung open. There stood Dad in the doorway. A lock of his strawberry-blond hair fluttered slightly in the breeze.

"Shay, honey, it's so good to see you. We've missed you so much." He pulled her in for a bearhug.

"I've missed you too, Dad."

"Come inside and sit down. You must be exhausted."

Unlike Shay's relationship with her mom, the bond she had with her father, Arthur, was solid. He was a construction worker and the kindest man she knew. She always looked up to him.

"Let me get these for you." Arthur took her bags and set them next to the staircase. Then he led her and Steve into the living room where Sherry was sitting in the recliner with her legs crossed. She wore a sunflower dress and black high heels, a typical blonde beauty, tall and leggy with shoulder length hair and chestnut brown eyes.

Sherry was every mother's dream for a daughter-in-law, and Janine loved her beyond words. She always said it was because of Sherry's "warm and loving demeanor," but Shay had a feeling it had less to do with her personality and more to do with her family. Sherry's father, Richard Douglas, was a renowned surgeon at Renwick General Hospital, and her mother, Joanna was the owner of a high-end clothing store.

Sherry got up from her seat and greeted her with a warm embrace. "It's so good to see you, Shay. You look great."

"Thanks. I love your dress." Shay took a seat on the couch.

As the four of them sat there, catching up, Shay looked around for her mother. "Hey, Dad. Where's Mom?"

"She went to the grocery store to get a few things for dinner, but she should be back soon."

Right at that moment, there was a sudden knock at the door. Arthur started to get up from his seat, but Shay motioned for him to sit down. "I'll get it, Dad. You just relax."

When she opened the door, her stomach did a cartwheel. Jason was standing on the porch, looking as handsome as ever. He was tall with short brown hair and hazel eyes. He was a talented artist and very sweet, which was an instant turn on for most of the girls in school, including Shay.

There was more to him than good looks and charm. Jason had a vulnerable side that few people knew about. When he was five, he lost his parents in a car accident, and as if that wasn't bad enough, he was in the backseat, and no matter how much he called out to them, they didn't answer his cries.

That tragedy had left a scar that would never truly heal, but he had an aunt who lived nearby, so he was spared the agony of foster care.

The fact that Jason trusted Shay enough to confide in her about something so big, only increased her feelings for him, but she was always too afraid to tell him how she felt because she knew the kind of girls he went for: tall, slim-figured brunettes with huge racks, while she was short and curvy with auburn hair and green eyes, and though she wasn't flat-chested, she was no Elvira.

"Shay Collins. It's been too long." He pulled her in for a hug, but though his cologne was intoxicating, she quickly stepped back.

"You only missed your wing woman,"

she joked. Pulling herself together, she did the best she could to not let her true feelings show.

"I've missed you."

"I haven't missed you, Jason," she said with a smirk.

"Yup. You haven't changed a bit, but still, it hasn't been the same without you around." He walked into the house.

For a minute, the two of them just stood there in the front hallway, staring at each other. She wished she had the courage to step closer and kiss him the way she did in her daydreams. Instead, she remained where she was until her father came over to greet him, who he always considered a second son.

"Jason, my boy, how are ya?"

"Hey, Mr. Collins," Jason said as he and Shay followed him into the living room. "How are you feeling? Are you taking it easy?"

"Have you met my wife? I don't have a choice in that matter."

What the hell? Her father was always a

healthy man; he never had any medical problems that she knew of. "What's Jason talking about, Dad?"

Arthur turned toward her and looked at her sweetly. "Now, honey, you wipe that worried look off your face right now. I'm fine. I had some chest pains a few months back at work. One of my co-workers called an ambulance. The doctor said I'd had a mild cardiac event caused by stress. I was able to go home after a couple of days."

"Why didn't anyone call me? I would have flown here to see you."

"Oh, honey, I know you would have, but you have such a busy life with your job and taking care of Chloe. Your mother thought it was best not to burden you with unnecessary worry."

That word, *burden*, angered Shay in a way that only her mother could spawn. Even if Shay couldn't have flown home, she would have appreciated a phone call, at least.

As her anger boiled to the surface, her mother walked through the front door, carrying a few grocery bags.

"That's my cue to leave," Jason said. Steve and Sherry followed him out the back door.

Shay stormed toward Janine. "You should have called me when Dad was in the hospital."

Janine glared at her. "Well, it's nice to see you too, Shay."

"I'm serious, Mom. Why didn't you tell me about Dad's heart attack?"

"Oh, Shay, stop acting like such a drama queen. You were busy living your life in New York, and I had everything under control. Besides, you wouldn't have come home."

"Don't do that. We aren't in the courtroom, so stop talking like a lawyer and be my mother for once."

Janine scoffed. "And what's that supposed to mean?"

"Ever since I was a kid, any time we disagreed, you would channel your inner lawyer and make the entire argument my fault. You could never admit when you were wrong."

"That's ridiculous. I just state the facts and the fact is, you haven't visited since you moved to New York. If you cared as much as you say you do, you wouldn't need an emergency to come home."

"You think I don't care about my family? If that was truly the case, you wouldn't hear from me at all."

"I never hear from you," Janine shouted. "The only time you call is to talk to your father. We may talk a minute but that's it." Janine looked hurt as a tear ran down her cheek, but Shay knew better than to fall for her mother's act; she was an expert at deceiving her opponents.

She saw her father stand up from his chair, as if to intervene, but she wasn't finished with her mother. "All you've ever done, my entire life, is insult me. After years of your endless verbal torment, I decided to put an end to it."

"Okay, ladies, calm down." Dad took the grocery bags from Janine. "Take a breather before someone says something that can't be taken back."

Shay ignored his advice. "Oh, and for your information, Mom, I did come back to California a few months ago."

Janine frowned. "You did not."

Shay felt the heat of her repudiation. "Chloe and I came back for a few days to visit some old friends. We even stopped by the house to see Dad when you weren't home. So you see, Mom, I didn't want to be around you."

Open-mouthed Arthur looked like he was going to intervene again, but Shay stopped him. "It's okay, Dad, I'm done." She grabbed her purse. "Can I borrow your car for a bit? I need to get some air."

Arthur nodded. "I think that's a good idea." He took his wife by the hand and led her into the living room.

Once Shay got in the car, she took a deep breath, and before she knew it, tears were streaming down her face. She couldn't believe all the awful things she'd said to her mother. Yeah, they'd had a lot of brawls over the years, but Shay always knew where to draw the line, but tonight, she'd lost all control. Right now, all she wanted to do was go home and hold Chloe close to her.

Chapter 4

Shay knew she couldn't sit in the driveway all night, so she drove to *Cups Up*, a bar down the street from her parents' house. When she walked in, she heard a familiar voice call out. "Shay."

It was Matt, bulling toward her, the beer in his mug sloshing out.

Seriously? After everything that's happened, he's at a fucking bar again?

"Listen, Shay, *hic*, we need to talk."

"Matt, I'm not in the mood right now. I'm having a bad night and a conversation with you will just make it worse."

"But we haven't talked since the incident, and I really...really think, for Chloe's sake, we need to make an effort with each...other."

"Incident, really? I let you watch our daughter for the weekend because you said you were in AA. You told me you'd been sober for months but instead, you got sloppy drunk in the middle of the afternoon and didn't see Chloe run out of the house. For God's sake, Matt, she was wandering around in traffic, crying her heart out, scared to death, and here you are drinking again. What the fuck is wrong with you?"

"So you got full custody of Chloe, I deserved that, but you took her to New York. Now I can only see her when a court-appointed social worker is there to supervise, and...and I'm the bad guy? God, Shay. I make one mistake and get labeled a drunk who can't take care of his own kid."

"First of all, that wasn't the *first* mistake you made. It was just the topper. And second, you don't make mistakes like that when there's a child involved."

"Bullshit. You know I'm a good dad."

"Matt, I'm not going to argue with you here. This conversation is over. Goodbye." She brushed past him and took a seat at the bar.

The bartender stepped up. "Whatcha drinking tonight?"

"Apple martini, please." With the way she was feeling, she could have probably bought out the bar, but she didn't want to become a lush like her ex-husband. What upset her the most when it came to Matt was that he wasn't always a drunk. When she first met him, they were in their freshman year of college at UCLA, both studying English. They connected right away and hung out almost every day. It wasn't until their sophomore year that Matt finally asked her out.

He was a talented athlete, sophisticated, and very charming. He was also very handsome: average height and a bit on the husky side, with a thick head of blond hair and green eyes. When they were together, she felt safe. He was the only guy, besides Jason, that she saw in her future.

It was on their six-month anniversary that Matt proposed, and he made sure to make it a memorable experience. He took her to a fancy French restaurant, which gave her the opportunity to dress up. She felt like a true princess in a beautiful blue dress Matt had purchased for her. They had a three-course meal and then, right as they were about to leave, Matt got down on one knee and proposed. She was completely surprised. The feelings she had for Jason were overwhelmed by Matt's romantic appeal. She was completely enamored and willing to start a life with him.

It wasn't until after they got married, that she began to see a different side of Matt, but now was not the time to think back on the problems of her marriage; it would only make her angrier. She slid her drink aside and ordered fried pickles and a diet soda. An hour later, she picked up her purse, headed for the car, and drove back to her parents' house.

Chapter 5

When Shay got home, the house was dark. Inside, she heard the soft hum of the TV. She expected to find her dad asleep on the couch, but when she entered the living room, she saw Jason sitting there, holding a glass of soda.

"Hey, why are you still here?"

He stood, the gentleman that he was. "Arthur called me, told me you were upset when you left, so I came back to make sure you were okay."

She gave him a warm smile. This was a reason she loved him. If only she had the nerve to tell him.

"I'm feeling much better now. Where are my parents?"

"Your dad thought it was best to give you and your mom some space for a while, so he took her out to dinner and a movie."

She chuckled. "He always knew how to

contain the fire."

Jason motioned to the couch. "Feel like watching a movie?"

"What should we watch?"

"Lady's pick."

"How about *Saw*?" She liked the idea of being scared and cuddling up next to him.

"Really?"

"Yep." She selected the movie from the bookshelf and popped it into the DVD player. Then she sat down with Jason and scooted close to him.

During the movie, she used some of the gory scenes to her advantage by screaming and hiding her face in his chest. He laughed and put his arm around her, his eyes never leaving the screen.

Shay, on the other hand, took the moment to look up at the man she always loved and longed to kiss.

Jason waved his hand in front of her face. "Hello? Shay, did you hear me?"

"Huh? Sorry. What?"

He laughed. "I should get going."

"The movie isn't over yet."

"You're zoning out. It's been a long day for you."

"Okay. Thanks for looking out for me."

"Of course." He walked to the front door. "See you later."

"Bye. Drive safe." She plopped down in front of the TV again.

Minutes later, her parents walked in.

"How was dinner?" she called out.

"Delicious." Her father patted his stomach. "If you'll excuse me, though, I'm going to head upstairs."

"I'll be up in a few minutes," Janine said.

Arthur was already halfway up the stairs when Janine walked into the living room and offered a brown paper bag to Shay. "A peace offering."

Shay opened the bag to find a piece of chocolate cream pie, her favorite dessert from the Red Oak Diner. "Thank you."

"Believe it or not, Shay, I don't enjoy fighting with you."

"Me either."

"Truce then?"

"We can try."

The corners of Janine's mouth twitched to form a small smile. "Okay. Good night."

"Good night."

Shay took her piece of pie into the kitchen and grabbed a fork. Maybe this weekend wouldn't be so bad, after all.

Chapter 6
Friday

When the sound of her mother's yelling woke Shay up, she decided to get out of the house. As she was heading out the door, she caught part of Janine's rant on the phone.

"If you do that, you will live to regret it."

Shay had no idea what her mom was steamed about, but she felt bad for whoever was on the other end of the line. She walked to the Short Stack Diner, about a mile away. When she got there, the place was packed, but the chocolaty goodness of the diner's big fluffy pancakes would be well worth the wait.

She took a seat in the atrium, eagerly waiting her turn for a table, and moments later, felt a tap on her shoulder. When she turned around, she was surprised to see

Corrine Davis, her brother's ex-girlfriend.

Corrine was a petite redhead with hazel eyes and cute freckles on her nose. She and Steve dated all through high school, but she broke up with him in the middle of their senior year. She even transferred to another school.

Despite how things ended between them, Shay still liked her. They'd kept in touch for a while but lost contact after Corrine graduated and went on to the University of Arizona.

"Oh, my God, Corrine, how are you?" She stood to give her a hug.

"Still waiting tables but at a much better restaurant." She pulled out of the hug and sat down, placing her brown handbag on her lap.

Shay sat next to her. "Are you still living in Arizona?"

"Yeah. I'm visiting my parents for the weekend. My dad is here with me right now. He's parking the car. What brings you back to California?"

"Steve's wedding."

"Oh, that." Corrine smiled, but from the slant of her brows, Shay could tell it was forced.

Is she hurt that Steve had moved on?

That would be odd since she was the one who'd ended the relationship.

Corrine's father sauntered into the diner and smiled when he saw Shay. "It's good to see you, Shay. How is New York?"

"Great, Mr. Davis. I'm so surprised to see you guys."

"Your dad always brags about you. Takes a lot of courage to set out on your own, clear across country. He's very proud of you, and so am I."

"Thanks, Mr. Davis."

At that moment, Shay was called to a table. "Would you guys like to join me?"

"Sure, thanks," Corrine said.

They followed their waitress to the table, then Shay took Corrine's purse and set it next to hers on the extra chair. After they placed their order, they continued to catch up, talked about Corrine working her way through college and Shay's life in New York

City with Chloe and Caroline, but stayed away from the subject of Steve's wedding.

"Do you remember the first time you slept over at my house?" Corrine asked.

Shay smiled. "It was a school night and we stayed up past midnight, talking and laughing."

Corrine giggled. "My parents almost lost their voices from shouting 'Go to bed, girls.'"

Shay glanced at Joe Davis, who was chuckling behind a cupped hand, then: "It's so nice to see you girls talking like no time has passed."

"High school was a great time," Corrine said. Her voice was choked up, though, and tears welled in her eyes, but she took a deep breath and pulled herself together.

Their conversation was put on pause when their food came. Shay dug into her pancakes while Corrine tackled her veggie omelet, and Joe dove into his Western Scramble.

When their waitress came by with the check, Shay saw Joe reach for his wallet.

She motioned for him to stop. "I got it."

"Okay, but I'll get the next one."

"Fair enough."

Once they were outside, Joe pointed to his car. "Do you need a ride?"

"Thanks, but I need to walk off these pancakes."

Corrine reached into her purse and took out a pen and a piece of paper. "Here's my number. Keep in touch, okay?"

"You got it."

As Shay was walking back to the house, she thought about Corrine and how sad she looked at the mention of Steve's wedding. Shay always thought Corrine was perfect for Steve. They had similar personalities and could always make the other laugh. Shay couldn't remember a time when they weren't smiling and cuddling like smitten puppies.

Only a few months after she'd dumped him, he'd started dating Sherry, which made Shay think that Sherry might have been a rebound relationship, but she never questioned Steve about it. He was always a standup guy, and Shay trusted that he wouldn't lead a girl on, just to get over someone else. Still, seeing Corrine again made her wonder if Steve was marrying the right woman.

Chapter 7

Shay was exhausted, not to mention full, when she returned from her walk back home. She wanted nothing more than to sit and relax with a bottle of water. When she entered the kitchen, "Where'd you escape to?" her dad asked.

"The Short Stack Diner." Shay glanced at her mother, at the sink, washing dishes.

"What?" Her mother turned to her. "You're only here for two days and can't bother to eat breakfast with us?"

So much for last night's peace offering.

"Excuse me for wanting to eat in peace without listening to you yell into the phone."

Arthur glowered at Janine. "Who were you yelling at?"

"Shay is just being dramatic. I wasn't yelling at anyone. I was simply having a spirited discussion with someone I used to work with." Janine glared at Shay as if she'd let slip some entrusted secret. It was the first time she ever looked uncomfortable during a conversation, like she'd just told a lie on the stand, under oath.

Rather than cross-examine her, Shay chose to change the subject. "Guess who I saw at the diner."

"Santa Claus?" her dad quipped.

"Corrine and Joe Davis."

Arthur showed her a warm smile; he always had a soft spot for Corrine. "The last time I spoke with Joe, he said she was doing very well in Arizona."

"She seems happy, but she looked hurt when I mentioned Steve's wedding. After that, I didn't mention it again."

Janine scoffed. "I assume she's still waiting tables for a living."

"She has bills to pay, Mom. And she managed to pay for school without any help from her parents. I admire her for that."

Janine glared at her with demeaning eyes. "Of course you would." She stormed out.

Janine believed Steve was going to

make a mark in the world, and he needed someone who was just as successful by his side. In her eyes, a waitress who came from a mediocre family would never be good enough for her exceptional son.

Janine was right about one thing; Steve did become very successful. After high school, he attended Yale University, where he received a bachelor's degree in web design and later a master's degree in business management. Now he works for a company that designs websites for major businesses all over the country. Shay had no reason to think that Corrine or her family would have held Steve back.

The weird thing was, that up until Shay was ten years old, Joe and his wife Elaine were good friends with her parents. They had known each other for years before she was even born. But one day, out of the blue, Janine had decided she was too good for their company and cut them out of her social life. Any time Arthur got together with the Davises, Janine made herself scarce until they left.

Shay's phone rang. It was Caroline.

"Why didn't you call me yesterday?"

"I completely forgot. How are you doing? I hope Chloe isn't driving you too crazy."

Caroline sighed. "Chloe's been an angel, but I'm really stressed about something else right now."

"What's going on?"

"I talked to my mom a little while ago. She doesn't sound good. I thought moving her here and getting her away from her problems back home would help her, but she's still going downhill."

Shay felt bad for Caroline's mom. Mrs. Fisher was like a second mother. She was a good person, and up until seven months ago, she was a happily married woman of twenty-five years, but one day she came home to find her husband in bed with a co-worker. Come to find out, he'd been having that affair for over a year.

Mrs. Fisher had filed for divorce, as if that would solve her problem, but her husband's deceit left her broken beyond repair. She sank into a deep depression, rarely leaving her home, and she distanced herself from everyone around her. Knowing she needed help, Caroline had convinced her mother to pack her things and move to New York.

The move seemed to help, at first. Mrs. Fisher started to act like her happy self again, but that soon changed when she received a few phone calls from Caroline's dad, begging for forgiveness. That's when her depression re-emerged.

"I know you're worried, Caroline, but it's going to take time for those wounds to heal. You've done everything you can do. You helped her get a new job and you found a therapist for her to talk to. All you can do now is be there for her while she works through the heartbreak."

"I know, you're right. It's just hard for me to see her so sad and defeated. Anyway, enough about me and my problems. How's everything going on your end?"

"There was drama with my mom and a confrontation with Matt, but the silver lining is that I hung out with Jason."

"Oh, I forgot. He's Steve's best man."

"And he still looks amazing."

Caroline giggled. "So...are you finally going to tell him how you feel?"

"No." Just then, Shay got another call.

"Can we talk later? Jason is calling me."

"Tell him I said hi."

"Give Chloe a hug and kiss for me." She switched to the incoming call. "Hey, Jason, what's up?"

"I was just wondering. Do you have any plans for tonight?"

"I'm going to hang out with my mom and get tortured to death. Why?"

"Let's grab dinner at Al's Pizza Joint and maybe catch a movie."

That came as a surprise that gave her heart a skip. "Are you asking me out on a date?"

"Sure. We can call it that."

A date? Is he serious? "What time?"

"I'll pick you up at seven."

"See you then." As she hung up, her tummy fluttered with butterflies at the very thought of kindling a romance with Jason.

Chapter 8

It took Shay an hour to get ready for her dinner date with Jason. Since she had no idea what tonight would bring, she needed the perfect outfit that screamed *friendly outing* but whispered *sexy date*.

After she spent twenty minutes combing through her suitcase, she finally decided on her powder blue V-neck sweater with black lace trim and light blue skinny jeans. To make the outfit pop, she wore short black boots with two-inch heels.

Of course, once the outfit was chosen, she needed the right amount of makeup to accentuate her features. She applied her light brown eye shadow and black eyeliner, then used her rosy red lipstick as the final touch, and then headed downstairs.

As soon as she reached the foot of the steps, Jason rang the doorbell. As usual, there were no complaints with his appearance, as he subtly exposed his alluring physique in dark blue jeans and a navy-blue t-shirt that showed off his perfect tan and muscular arms. When he saw Shay, he gave her a smile, and she could have sworn his eyes traveled down her body, but that could have been wishful thinking.

"You look great," he said, still smiling.

"Thanks, so do you." She returned his smile.

She wanted to make a move on him right then and there, but since she was unsure of his intentions, she ignored her womanly needs and simply followed him to his car.

Once at the restaurant, he ordered their old favorite, two Pepsis and a medium Meat Lovers pizza, then they began to catch up.

"So, what have you been up to since I left California?" she asked. "Are you still teaching?"

"Only parttime now. It took me forever, but I finally got my artwork in a gallery."

She was excited for him but not surprised; she always knew he could make it in the art world. "That's fantastic. What gallery is it in?"

"Mine, actually. I decided I didn't just want people to see my work, I wanted to help promote the work of other aspiring artists. So, last year, a few months after you left, I decided to open Kent's Art Gallery. It took a while for everything to come together but it was worth it."

"Congratulations."

"If you want to check it out before you go back to New York, let me know."

Before she could say anything else, someone called her name. "Shay Collins, is that you? It's been so long."

Shay shifted in her seat. "Marc?" she asked when she saw the man standing behind her. Marc Phillips went to school with her and Jason, but she hadn't seen him since they graduated. She stood to hug him. "How are you?"

"I'm good, thanks. So, you two are tight, huh?"

"Oh, no. We're just grabbing dinner." She quickly corrected Marc's assumption.

Marc smiled. "I've got to run." He pulled a card from his pocket and handed it to her. "Call me if you want to get a drink sometime. See ya." He waved and left.

Shay caught Jason's eye; he was giving her a big smirk.

"That guy is still into you."

She scoffed and waved him off.

He maintained his sly smile. "Seriously? The dude was a brainiac who failed Geometry, just so you could tutor him."

"Huh?"

"Why do you seem so surprised? You were a total catch."

After they finished their pizza and left the restaurant, he drove to the movie theater. Right after he took his key out of the ignition, she grabbed his hand. "Wait."

"Everything okay?"

"There's something I've been wanting to tell you." Her heart began to race, and she was suddenly at a loss for words, so instead of trying to explain how she felt, she leaned in and kissed him...well...more of a peck, as she didn't throw herself at him like she wanted to.

He stiffened in surprise, or shock, she didn't know which, and pulled back.

Oh, oh. "I'm so sorry." She lowered her head to conceal the embarrassment in her eyes. Her impulsive decision had just backfired.

He placed a finger under her chin and gently lifted her eyes to meet his. "I didn't know you felt that way." He'd said that with a smile and in a voice so soft she was sure she'd melt in his arms.

"I've wanted to kiss you so many times."

"I wish you had." He slid his arms around her and gathered her in for another go at it, this time with parted lips and a meeting of their tongues in a dance as old as time. He smelled of sandalwood and vanilla, and his nearness sent a shiver down her spine as she melted in his embrace.

She'd dreamt of this moment for so long, and it was even better than she could have ever imagined.

***

Later, When Shay returned to her parents' house, she found her mother sitting alone in the living room. She was flipping through a floral-print photo album, and her eyes were red and puffy; she'd been crying for a while.

"Everything okay, Mom?"

"Huh? Oh, yeah." She was clearly startled by Shay's entrance. "I'm fine."

"You don't look fine."

"Leave me alone."

First, the angry phone call and now an emotional breakdown. There was something going on with her mother. She just wished they were close enough for her to open up about it.

Chapter 9
Saturday

When Shay woke up the next morning, her dad's car was gone, and her mom was doing something in the kitchen, so she decided to eat elsewhere; *Dunkin* would be a good place. She grabbed her purse and the newspaper that was resting on the coffee table and walked to the diner.

As she was working on a crossword between bites of her cinnamon raisin bagel, her phone rang. "Hello."

"Hey, it's Sherry. My bridesmaids and I are running over to Curly Q Salon to get our nails done. Do you want to meet us?"

"Would love to. See you soon."

Shay took a final bite of her breakfast then called a cab. She met up with Sherry and the other girls just as they were heading in.

"Shay, you already know my Maid of Honor, Christine. These are my bridesmaids, Brianna, Sandra, and Melanie."

"Nice to meet you all."

"You too," Brianna said.

The other two bridesmaids smiled and nodded in agreement, but they barely made eye contact with Shay.

"Glad you could make it," Christine said. Her smile looked forced, and her tone lacked sincerity.

She couldn't help but feel like an unwanted interloper, as she walked in with everyone. They got settled in their pedicure chairs and that's when the gossip started.

"You know who else I heard is getting married soon?" one girl said with a wicked grin. "Jennifer Taylor."

Brianna, the shortest of the bunch, chimed in. "Someone actually proposed to that tramp?"

Christine joined the childish chit chat. "I doubt it will last. Her groom was just as much a man-whore as she was a slut."

Shay couldn't believe how vicious these

girls sounded. It was like they were back in high school, bashing any girl they didn't like.

"Pleezzz," Sherry hissed. "Jennifer is a nun compared to Steve's ex-girlfriend, Corrine. That girl opened her legs for any boy that smiled in her direction."

"That's not true," Shay said in Corrine's defense.

Christine snickered. "I heard she got pregnant."

Brianna said, "That's why she had to change high schools."

Sherry examined her fingernails. "I wonder who knocked her up."

"Nobody," Shay insisted. "Gossip. That's all it is."

Sherry laughed. "But isn't it fun?"

Shay knew Corrine was never pregnant. Steve would have said something. She didn't want to listen to these snobby girls bash her good friend any longer. She pulled her feet out of the pedicure tub. "Go ahead. Have your fun. I'm outta here."

"Okee doke." Sherry flicked her fingers dismissively.

***

Shortly after Shay got back from the salon, she received a text from Corrine: *Want to meet for lunch?*

Shay: *I'll meet you at the mall.*

When Shay got to the mall, she saw Corrine standing outside. Her wavy red hair was blowing in the wind.

"Hey, Shay. I'm so happy you were able to meet up with me."

"Me too." She pulled Corrine in for a hug. "Let's go find a seat in the food court and have some much-needed girl-talk."

When they sat down, Corrine asked, "Are you okay?"

"I'm pissed at Sherry and her girlfriends. They were gossiping about you at the nail salon."

"Good or bad?"

"They were talking trash about you being pregnant."

Corrine took a deep breath. "Yeah, about that." She handed her a picture of an adorable little girl with curly red hair and deep blue eyes. "I have a nine-year old daughter, Alyssa."

Shay about fell out of her chair. The girls at the salon were right. She'd made a fool of herself. "Why didn't you tell me before? I didn't even know you were pregnant."

Corrine's face turned pale, as if she were about to confess to a murder. "She's Steve's daughter."

Shay felt faint. "No way. Steve would have told me—"

"I never told him."

The food court tilted. "You hid his daughter from him for *nine* years?"

"I had no choice."

"Of course you had a choice." She stood and turned to leave. "We're done talking."

"Please, Shay, let me explain."

She kept walking, got two tables away when she heard: "Your mother made me do it."

That hit her like a blow to the back of the head. She stopped cold, turned slowly, then stormed back to the table. "Oh, this better be good."

"When I found out I was pregnant, I told my mom. She told your mom. Boy did I get the third degree from her. She kept asking, *"How do I know it's Steve's?"* I told her I lost my virginity that night of the big snowstorm...when I stayed at your house."

"I remember that night. It was too dangerous to drive home in a blizzard."

"It was so cold outside, so warm in Steve's arms. It just sort of happened."

"I can't say I blame you, but how could you not tell him?"

"Your mom thought I wasn't good enough for Steve. She gave me a check for $10,000 to keep my mouth shut and never tell him about the baby."

Shay couldn't believe what she was hearing. Yes, Janine was a woman of power and control, but this went far beyond control; this was plain vile.

"When I refused the check, she ranted on about how my foolishness would ruin Steve's life and any chance he had of becoming successful. I told her Steve would love to be a father. That's when she turned my words to her advantage and insisted Steve would resent me and the baby for dashing his dreams."

"I get that, but, Corrine, you know Steve was completely in love with you. You broke his heart when you dumped him without as much as a what-for."

"I tried to set things right. A few months after Alyssa was born, I decided to tell Steve everything. He was visiting your parents for the weekend, so I drove to the house, but as soon as I pulled up, your mom ran outside to stop me. She told me how happy Steve was without me, and that if I said anything to him about Alyssa, she would make my life a living hell."

Just when Shay thought Janine had hit her ultimate low, she had pulled this stunt. "She seriously threatened you?"

"There's one thing I've learned about your mom, she never bluffs, so I enrolled in the University of Arizona. Got the hell out of town before your mom made good on her threat."

"She's pure evil...but why are you

telling me this now?"

"Alyssa has been asking about her dad. That's why we're here this weekend. I called your mom yesterday morning and I told her that I didn't care what she did to me, Steve was going to find out about Alyssa before he marries that bitch Sherry."

So it was Corrine who Mom was yelling at on the phone.

Shay reached over to take Corrine's hand. "I've always thought you were a better match for Steve than Sherry. It's not too late. I think you two might still have a chance."

"Thank you for understanding, Shay. You can keep your niece's picture. I have more."

Shay looked again at the picture of Alyssa. "Thanks. Now it's time I deal with my mother."

Chapter 10

Shay was on her way back to her parents' house to have it out with her mother, when her phone rang. "Hello?"

"Is this Shay Collins?"

"Yes. Who is this?"

"I'm calling from Renwick General Hospital. Matt Blanco was just admitted to the ER, and we found your contact information in his wallet."

A lump formed in her throat. "Thank you, I'm on my way."

There was a cop standing outside his room when she arrived.

"Excuse me, officer. This is my ex-husband's room. Could you please tell me what happened?" Shay wiped a few tears from her eyes.

"He crashed into a guard rail. No other cars were involved but the medics smelled alcohol on his breath."

Shay let out a deep sigh. "What's going to happen to him?"

"For now, he's under arrest for suspected drunk driving, unless a blood test comes back under the legal limit."

"Can I see him?"

The officer nodded.

She always knew that one day Matt's excessive drinking would catch up with him. It started shortly after Shay found out she was pregnant with Chloe, which was around the same time Matt lost his job. Shay tried to get him help, but he always insisted that he didn't have a problem.

When she walked in, Matt was lying there with a bandage around his head and oxygen tubes in his nose.

"Oh, Matt." Shay shook a finger at him. "Drunk driving? Really?"

"I had one drink, that's it."

"Save the bullshit for someone who doesn't know you, Matt. I spoke with the cop. He told me you were drunk. What the hell were you thinking? Drinking and driving? You're lucky no one else got hurt."

"See? It's not a big deal."

"Yeah, but what about the next time, huh? Matt, this is serious. You have an addiction, and you need help."

"Forget it, Shay. I'm not going to rehab."

"Whatever, Matt. The judge will decide."

He closed his eyes and turned his head away.

Shay left the room. Her fists were clenched, and her face was red with anger. She was ready for another fight. When she got back to the house, she pushed open the door to find Steve and Sherry doing a puzzle in the living room.

"Hey, Shay," Steve said. "You're just in time. We got the border done and now we need help with the ocean." He held up a box that had a picture of a sailboat with a blue hull set against a dark sea.

Shay slammed her purse on the living room chair. "Where's Mom?"

"What's wrong?" Steve got up and put his hand on her shoulder. "Are you okay?"

"No. I need to talk to Mom, and I don't

think Sherry should be here for this."

"She's family. Of course she should be here."

"Don't say I didn't warn you. Now where's Mom?"

"What's all the yelling?" Her mother came out of the kitchen, drying her hands on a dishtowel.

Shay charged toward her mother. "I just had a very interesting lunch with Corrine."

Janine's eyes grew wide with dread. "Shay, please, don't say another word."

Steve pressed between them. "Shay, what is your problem?"

She caught her brother's eye. "I'm sorry, Steve. Mom has gone too far this time. You and Corrine have a nine-year old daughter."

"What?" He wobbled as if the earth had moved under his feet.

"Her name is Alyssa."

"There's no way Corrine would have kept something like that from me."

"It's not Corrine's fault." She glared at her mother. "Isn't that right, Mom? It's your fault. You tried to pay her to keep quiet, and when she refused, you threatened to make her life a living hell. You thought he'd be better off without her."

Steve's face turned ashen. "Mom? Is that true?"

Arthur joined them in the living room. "I'm sure there's some misunderstanding, Shay. Your mom wouldn't do anything like that."

Sherry jumped in. "Your dad is right, Steve. Listen to yourself, Shay. You sound ridiculous."

Steve sat on the couch and buried his face in his hands. "I'm a dad?"

"No you're not," Janine said. "Corrine was nothing but trouble, I told you that."

Shay showed Steve the picture Corrine had given to her earlier. "Tell me that little girl doesn't look like you?"

Steve looked like he would bust out in tears at any second. "It can't be true." He looked at Janine. "Mom, tell her Corrine is lying. There's no way you would deny me my own daughter."

"Steve, that girl and her illegitimate

child were going to ruin your life, and since you were too blind to see the person she really was, I had to step in."

"How could you, Mom? For nine years you let me believe Corrine dumped me because she didn't love me when you had bullied her into breaking up with me."

"Don't be so dramatic, Steve. I simply did what I knew you were too weak to do. Look how successful you've become and look who you're going to marry. Sherry is far more well-suited for you than that girl ever was."

"I have to get out of here." Steve grabbed Sherry's hand and pulled her toward the door. Before he left, he looked at Shay. "Thank you. At least someone in this house loves me enough to be honest with me."

Arthur followed Steve and Sherry out the door.

Janine just stood there in complete silence, staring at Shay. This was Janine's way of saying, 'Get the hell out of my house before I force you out.'

Shay stormed upstairs to get dressed for, what was sure to be, a disastrous rehearsal dinner, then grabbed her purse and called a cab to drive her to Griffin Park, a playground that she and Steve often went to as kids. With the high level of chaos swirling around her, a little childlike fun was just what she needed.

When she got there, she paid the driver then walked to the swing-set and kicked off her black heels before she sat in the swing. With her purse in her lap, she dragged her feet back, pushed herself forward and extended her legs out. Like riding a bike, she hadn't forgotten how to get the swing up to speed.

Though she enjoyed the up and down motion of the swing, she couldn't help but think about Steve. She could still see the shock on his face and the devastation in his eyes when she told him of their mother's betrayal. The part that bothered her the most was Sherry's lack of emotional reaction. She didn't seem angry or even worried that Steve had a daughter with another woman.

Shay slowed the swing and grabbed her phone out of her purse. She called Steve. "Are you still getting married?"

"Sherry and I had a long talk. We still want to get married tomorrow, but after the rehearsal, the dinner is cancelled. We need tonight to ourselves."

"What about Corrine and Alyssa?"

"Obviously, I want to be a part of my daughter's life. I called Corrine and we're going to set up a time to meet and figure out a plan that works for everyone."

"And Sherry's okay with all of this?"

"Of course. She knows I love her, and she understands that I need to get to know Alyssa."

"And what about Mom?"

"I told her not to come to the wedding, but she'll probably show up anyway."

"True. I'll see you tomorrow."

She had one more call to make. "Hey, Jason. I really need to see you. Can you come and get me? I'm at Griffin Park."

"I'm on my way."

Chapter 11

Once they got to Jason's place, they took a seat on his black leather sofa where Shay filled him in on everything that occurred earlier.

"That explains a lot," Jason said, looking just as surprised as Shay did when she first found out about Alyssa. "I can't believe Steve has a daughter."

"I'm still trying to wrap my head around it. She has Steve's eyes and Corrine's cute little nose."

"What's he going to do?"

"He called Corrine. They're going to work something out so that he can get to know Alyssa. Personally, I think he should call off the wedding. "

"I thought you liked Sherry."

"I was wrong about her. Corrine is a better match for Steve."

"I told him he should fight for her, but

he was too hurt to listen. I don't think he ever got over losing her."

She leaned in close and whispered softly in his ear. "Enough talking."

She pressed her lips against his. Jason then looped his arm around her waist and pressed his body against hers, while gently caressing her thigh. His hand slowly moved up her body, giving her chills of desire.

"Do you want to take this to the bedroom?"

"If you have to ask, I'm doing something wrong."

Jason picked her up like she weighed nothing and hurried up the stairs. He placed her feet back down and guided her to the bed. Her heart began to race. He quickly removed his dark blue button-down shirt, exposing his perfect chest and brawny muscles. She turned her back to him so he could unzip her red cocktail dress and unclip her black-laced bra. She turned back to face him and unzipped his pants. They kicked off their shoes, and before long, they were entwined on the bed, with every stitch of their clothing scattered on the floor.

Jason took a moment to gaze into her eyes before their bodies melded together as one.

***

When Shay woke up the next morning, she got out of Jason's bed and collected her clothes from the floor.

Jason pushed the sheet down off his chest. "Stay for a few more minutes." He stole her bra and twirled it like a lasso.

She climbed on the bed and grabbed for it but missed. "We have to go get ready for the wedding."

"Come get it." His devious smile tempted her to repeat last night's lovemaking. "You don't have to be there early. It's not like you're in the wedding party."

"But you are, so quit clowning around and get dressed. You have to drive me home so I can shower and change clothes." This time she grabbed the bra, but instead of letting it go, he pulled her down on top of him.

"Fine," he whispered. "But the ride will cost you one more kiss."

She pressed her lips to his and invited his tongue to play. Passions flared up again, tempting her to change her mind.

True to his word, he released the bra.

She sat up and slipped it on, every motion under his watchful eye. As she slid into her dress, she glanced back over her shoulder, smiled, and gave him a wink. He sat up without hesitation and grabbed hold of the zipper. For a minute, he just held it, kissing her shoulder, tempting her once more. Finally, he pulled up the zipper then retrieved his clothes from the floor.

"This wedding should be interesting," he said, as they walked to his car.

***

When Shay drove her dad's car into the church parking lot, she saw people were already walking in. After she parked, she headed for the church doors to join the procession. When she entered, she was graced by the sound of beautiful organ music that echoed through the rectory. As she listened to the organist play, she looked around, admiring the assortment of colors on the stained glass windows.

She was about to take her seat when the Maid of Honor, Christine, rushed up to her and grabbed her by the arm.

"Sherry wants to see you before the ceremony starts."

"Oh, oh." *This can't be good.* Shay followed her at a quick pace. When they entered the bridal room, Christine left right away.

Sherry wore a strapless white gown with a ruffled skirt and a two-tier scallop-edged veil. However, her red-faced scorn stole all of her bridely beauty.

"What do you want, Sherry?"

"Everything is ruined, thanks to you."

"Steve needed to know what our mother hid from him."

"You opened your big mouth and managed to insert that awful Corrine into our marriage. Now Steve wants to get to know the child, which means she's going to be a constant wedge between us."

"First of all, Sherry, that child has a name, Alyssa. She's Steve's daughter, and he has a right to be a part of her life."

"You don't get it, Shay. Corrine is going to manipulate her way back into Steve's heart. I can never trust him to be faithful to me. Why couldn't you just butt out? We had everything under control."

"We?"

"Your mother and I. She's a very smart woman—"

"You knew about Alyssa?"

"Back in high school, before she transferred, I saw her in the girls' room, standing in front of the mirror. She was looking down at her stomach and crying. I put two and two together. She had been going with Steve so he probably got her pregnant."

"And you said nothing to her?"

"What was I going to say? We weren't friends, but after Steve and I got together, I thought she could become a problem. That's when I confided in your mom, and she assured me that the situation had been taken care of."

"I can't believe you knew this whole time and never told him."

"Come on, Shay. It's not like I committed murder or something. I was saving Steve from the biggest mistake of his life, sleeping with that whore. What was he thinking?"

Shay wasn't about to stand there and listen to her bad-mouth Corrine. "You're a hateful, spiteful bitch like my mother. Steve's got to know you were in cahoots with my mom before it's too late."

"Haven't you caused enough trouble, Shay?"

"I'm just getting started." When she opened the door to leave, Steve was standing there. The expression on his face was akin to the Grim Reaper's.

"I heard it all, Shay. Now give me a moment alone with Sherry."

She stepped out of the room. "I'm so sorry, Steve."

"I'm not." He charged into the room with Sherry and shut the door.

Shay didn't want to stay in that church a minute longer, but to avoid a scene, she found a seat in one of the crowded pews and listened to the organist play the death march, or so it seemed.

It didn't take long before Steve entered the chapel and called for everyone's attention. "Thank you all for coming, but the wedding is off. I'm sorry. Have a safe trip home."

Steve marched down the aisle quickly with his head down to avoid the stares of his shocked guests. As soon as he walked out the door, Janine stormed up to Shay, and with a look of pure hatred in her eyes, delivered a hard slap to Shay's face then stalked away.

Shay sat there, too stunned to move, as did others who'd witnessed Janine's fury.

Jason appeared from the haze and took her hand. "Let's get out of here."

Chapter 12

Jason drove to Betsy G's Café for a late breakfast. After he parked the car, he looked at Shay. "Before we go in, I just want to make sure you're okay."

"I feel a little guilty. I mean, I *am* the reason Steve isn't married right now. Maybe Sherry and my mother were right. I should have minded my own business."

"Don't blame yourself. Sherry and your mom made their bed and now they must lie in it. You're the reason Steve can be a part of his daughter's life. Being able to experience that kind of bond is a wonderful gift that not everyone gets."

"You should have seen the way my mother looked at me. It was like she was disowning me right then and there."

"I know you and your mom have a lot of issues, but I always felt that, deep down, there was love between you. You're the only one she's never been able to control or manipulate, and I think that kills her."

Jason's words gave her a sense of relief. Although Janine drove her crazy at times, she was still her mother and, in a way, she was the reason Shay was strong and assertive. She sighed. "Maybe you're right."

"Of course I'm right," Jason replied with a smug smile. "Now let's go inside and eat. I don't know about you but I'm starving."

Once they were seated and placed their order, Jason looked at Shay. "Do you think Steve went to see Corrine?"

"I think he's too angry to talk to anyone."

"I can't imagine what's going through his head right now."

As Shay was about to speak, their food arrived. Too hungry to make conversation, they ate in silence. When they were done, Jason paid the bill and they left. He opened the car door for her. "You ready to go home?"

"Not really, but I can't hide from my mother forever."

"I think I know how to buy you a little more time."

"Yeah? How?"

"You'll see. Just get in the car and close your eyes."

"Okay." She loved his confidence, so she closed her eyes, and after about a seven-minute drive, he put the car in park.

He got out and opened her door. "Okay, you can open them now."

Shay was speechless when she saw where Jason had taken her.

"Oh my God, your art gallery. It looks amazing." Shay got out of the car and took a minute to admire the outside of the building, grey, with *Kent's Art Gallery* written above in black lettering. Under the name was a painting of a beautiful snowy mountain top resting against a light blue sky.

When they walked in, each wall had a wonderful display of artwork. Some pieces were images of people, others were depictions of famous landmarks, but there was one piece that really caught her eye. It was of a woman standing barefoot on the beach, facing the ocean, and wearing a yellow flowy dress. In one hand she held a pair of brown sandals, in the other, she held the hand of a little girl, who pointed at a flock of seagulls that hovered above the water. She didn't need to look at the artist's name to know who painted it.

"This one's yours, isn't it?" she asked with a knowing smile.

"How did you know?"

"You always had a way of combining people and places into your artwork so it always looks real."

"You were my inspiration."

She set her head against his chest and savored his warmth. "Despite everything that's happened this weekend, I'm really glad I came back to California. I just wish this didn't have to end." She felt disappointed. Though she wanted to get back home to Chloe, she didn't want to say goodbye to Jason.

"Why does it have to end?"

"You know why. You live here, I live in New York, and long-distance relationships never work out. We tried that once, remember?"

Jason didn't give up. "Shay, I finally have you back in my life and we've got this really great thing going for us. I don't think we should let go so hastily."

"So, you're saying we should try long-distance again?"

"Why not?"

"I don't have a good feeling about it."

"Shay, I know you're worried, but I really think we can make it work this time."

"How do you figure?"

"This time I'm completely in love with you."

"I love you too." She wrapped her arms around him and gave him a steamy kiss. They'd waited so long for this relationship to happen. She wasn't ready to give it up either.

Jason took her hand, and they walked back to his car. When they got in, Shay's mind drifted back to Steve. When he left the church, there was so much pain in his eyes. She had never seen him look so defeated;

she needed to make sure he was okay, and she had a feeling she knew where he had gone. "Hey, Jason, before you take me home, can we make one more stop?"

"Sure. Where?"

"There's this place in the woods that Steve and I used to go to whenever things got tough. I think he might be there now."

"Just tell me where to go."

When they arrived, Steve's car was parked nearby and he was standing by the water, skipping stones.

"Do you want me to wait here?"

"No. I'll have Steve bring me back when we're ready. Thanks for the ride."

"I'll talk to you later."

She got out, and as soon as he drove off, she walked to Steve. "I knew you'd be here." She placed a sympathetic hand on his shoulder.

"Sorry about the wedding."

"How are you holding up?"

"Honestly? I'm hurt, but mostly I feel like a fool. Sherry betrayed me. How could I not see the type of person she really was?"

"Don't be so hard on yourself. She fooled me too."

"Our whole relationship was built on a lie. I don't even know who she is anymore."

"Sherry should have told you about Corrine's pregnancy, but she wasn't the one who made Corrine break up with you or ran her out of town. That was all mom."

"I don't know how I can look at her again. And let's not forget Corrine. I loved her, I trusted her, and look how she repaid me."

"Put yourself in her shoes. She was seventeen and just found out she was going to be a mother. To top that off, our mom bribed her and convinced her that she and the baby would be a burden on you. That's a lot for a young woman to deal with."

"She should have told me."

"She tried."

"Really?"

"After Alyssa was born, Corrine drove to the house, but mom came out and threatened to ruin her life before she could tell you."

Steve stared out at the clear blue water resting ahead of them. "At this point, nothing should surprise me."

"So maybe go easy on her?"

Steve gave a simple nod. "Thanks for checking on me."

"You're my brother. I love you. Corrine loves you. Alyssa's going to love you. Nothing else matters anymore."

Chapter 13

After Steve dropped her off, Shay walked into her parents' house and found her father sitting alone in the living room, sipping from a can of beer.

"Dad, you okay? Where's Mom?"

Her father sighed deeply. "I told her to leave."

"Wow, I'm sorry dad. That must have been an awful decision to make."

"I can't get over what she did to Steve, and slapping you in church was the last straw. That's not the woman I married."

"I'm so sorry. I just wanted Steve to know the truth. I didn't really think of the consequences."

Arthur looked at her and smiled. "Oh, honey, I don't blame you for any of this. You did the right thing. That's how you've always been, and I love that about you."

Shay found solace in those words. She

could handle her mother being angry with her, but she would never be the same if her father hated her too.

"Thank you, Dad. You have no idea how much that means to me." She wrapped her arms around him, and after a few minutes, she pulled back and looked at him again. "Can I ask you a question?"

"Of course."

"Was Mom always like this?"

"If you're asking if she's always been strong, stubborn, and over-protective, then yes. But you must understand something about your mom. Growing up, she never had anyone to look out for her."

"What do you mean?"

"Your grandfather worked nights, so he spent most of the day catching up on sleep, and let's just say, your grandmother thought criticism was a good way to build character."

"Okay, that sucks, but it doesn't excuse what she put Steve and Corrine through."

"Shay, what she did was awful, but what I'm saying is that, in her mind, she was protecting Steve."

"I don't know, Dad. All I see when I look at Mom is someone who constantly judged me and tried to control my life. There's a difference between being overprotective and just plain cruel."

"Hang on a second." Her dad frowned. "I think you're forgetting that the qualities you hate so much about your mother are what kept you from getting expelled for decking Dina Larson."

Shay remembered the time she'd stood up to the school's biggest bully, and Mom had her back in the principal's office.

"You're right. What are you going to do now?"

"I don't know."

"Where's Mom?"

"She's staying at the Renwick Inn. Room 312. We're taking a break from each other. That's all I can handle for the time being."

Seeing the sadness in her father's eyes, she wanted to do something to make things better for him, but she knew only time could do that. She gave him a hug. "I love you, Dad."

"I love you too, sweetheart." His eyes welled with tears. "I'll be fine, don't you worry. Go upstairs and pack. You have an early flight tomorrow."

Chapter 14
Monday

Shay woke to the smell of her father's famous eggs and bacon wafting through the house.

"Aww, Dad, you didn't have to make me breakfast," she yelled as she rushed down the stairs, but when she entered the kitchen, Arthur wasn't there. He had, however, made a plate for her as well as a fresh pot of coffee.

Just as she sat down to start eating, her phone rang. She didn't recognize the number. "Hello?"

"This is a collect call from the city jail. Do you accept the charges?"

It must be Matt. "Yes."

"Hello, Shay."

"Matt, if you called to argue, I'm hanging up."

"Relax. I just want to talk."

"I'm listening." She took a bite of her eggs and washed it down with a sip of coffee.

"You were right. I have a drinking problem."

"Why the sudden change in attitude?"

"Being arrested gave me a new perspective."

"Are you in a lot of trouble?"

"I'm here for three more days and I have to pay a hefty fine. They also suspended my license for a year."

"It's good to hear you acknowledge that you have a problem."

"Yeah, I'm going to start attending AA meetings."

Shay couldn't believe it. This wouldn't be the first time Matt had lied to her. "If you're serious about getting help, then I'm proud of you."

"I've never been more serious about anything in my life. I know I failed as a husband, but I'm going to make sure I don't fail as a father. I don't want to let Chloe down like I did with you."

"Matt, you made some mistakes when you drank but I always knew how much you love our daughter."

"So...if I get my act together, do you think I'll be able to see Chloe without the social worker around? I miss having one on one time with her."

"That's up to the judge, but if you stay sober, I think something can be worked out."

"You have no idea how much it means to hear you say that. Have a safe flight, Shay."

"Thanks. I'm available if you ever need to talk."

After she got off the phone, she finished her breakfast. She felt like her visit to California would have a positive ending. Now all she needed was to patch things up with her mother, not for herself, so much, but for Alyssa. That little girl deserved to have both sets of grandparents in her life, not only on Corrine's side of the family, but Steve's as well. She realized it would be like tiptoeing across quicksand, but it would be worth a try.

When her taxi arrived, the driver got out and loaded her suitcase in the trunk. "Where am I taking you this morning?"

"LAX, but first I need to stop by the Renwick Inn."

The driver stopped at the front entrance.

She got out. "I'll be right back."

"The meter's running, lady. Take your time."

She headed to the third floor, but when the elevator doors opened, she felt as if she were stuck in that quicksand. Her feet felt heavy as she walked to room 312. It wasn't too late to leave and never look back.

She took a breath and knocked on the door.

"Who is it?"

"It's me, your daughter."

The door flew open. "What are you doing here?"

"I came to talk about Alyssa."

Janine glared at her with tear-reddened eyes. "You're wasting your time. Don't you have a plane to catch?"

"The cab's waiting downstairs. Mom, this is important. Alyssa's not only Steve's daughter, she's your granddaughter. You should care about her as much as you care about Chloe."

"I don't, so spare me a long speech on how horrible a person I am."

"I'm not here to criticize you. I just want to show you what you're denying." Shay reached into her pocket then handed her mother Alyssa's picture. "This is your granddaughter. You may not like Corrine but don't take it out on Alyssa. For her sake, can't you make peace with her mother?"

Janine looked at the picture for a few seconds then offered it back to Shay.

"Keep it. I've got to go. And good luck with Dad."

The door closed.

Once she was back in the cab and on her way to the airport, Shay thought about the conversation she had with her mother, which triggered a pleasant flashback.

She was in the fifth grade and had just brought home her first straight-A report card. She'd burst through the front door, beaming with pride as she ran to show it to her mother. Janine smiled and gave her a warm hug, sweetly whispering in her ear, "I'm so proud of you, my angel."

That day was the nicest memory she had with her mother, but it was also one of the few good ones. It was as if the rest of her life never measured up to that one report card. Every achievement thereafter was dismissed, and though she had graduated high school with a 3.7 GPA and moved on to college where she'd earned a bachelor's degree in English, and later, a master's degree in creative writing, her mother's enthusiasm would have been appropriate for a stranger.

Chapter 15

Shay woke up Tuesday morning, wishing she could postpone her return to work. She wanted nothing more than to have extra mommy-daughter time with Chloe. But she forced herself out of bed, got ready for work, then helped Chloe get ready for pre-school.

After Shay entered her cubicle, Tony greeted her with a smile and a bouquet of red roses. "Morning, beautiful. How was your weekend?"

She took the flowers. "Thank you, Tony. How sweet of you." She glanced around for inquisitive ears. "We need to talk."

"What is it?"

"I've really enjoyed the last few months with you, but when I was in California, I reconnected with someone from my past."

His smile faded. "Oh. What's his name?"

"Jason."

"So, what now?"

"I can't see you anymore, you know, after work."

"I can't say I'm not disappointed. I was hoping this fling could turn into something more."

"You're a good guy, Tony. You'll find the right gal someday."

"I want you to be happy." Tony gave her a hug and a kiss on the cheek, then walked away, leaving her with feelings of extreme guilt. This made it hard for her to get through the next few hours of work, until she went on her lunch break. Between eating her sandwich and sending text messages to Jason, she observed Lila O'Connor shamelessly putting the moves on Tony.

Yeah. He would be just fine.

After work, Shay picked up Chloe from pre-school, and they spent the rest of the day watching TV and playing games before dinnertime. By the end of the night, Shay was exhausted, so she went to bed shortly after tucking Chloe in.

Around midnight, a ringing phone awoke her. Through sleep bleary eyes she examined the caller ID. It was her mom.

"Mom? Have you thought about what I said?"

"It's your father...he's gone, Shay."

"Gone? Where?"

"He's dead," she cried.

Shay fought back tears of her own. "What happened?"

"He called me at the inn...said he was feeling dizzy...chest pains. I rushed to the house...took him to the ER..." Janine's voice shook as she struggled to get her words out. "The doctors rushed him to surgery. Shay, they did all they could...but they couldn't save him."

"He was a healthy man. How could this happen?"

"He was a stubborn man. 'No big deal...don't bother the 911 people. They have more important things to do.'"

"Mom, I'm so sorry. I'll catch the first flight back to California."

"That's not necessary, Shay. Your

brother will help me with the arrangements. I'll call you as soon as the funeral has been finalized."

"If you need me to do anything, anything at all, we're just a plane ride away."

"Would you mind writing the eulogy?"

"Are you sure?"

"You and your dad had a special bond. I think he would want you to speak for him."

"I'll get started on it right away." She switched her tear-soaked cell phone to the other ear. "I can't believe he's gone."

"Me either." Janine hesitated for a moment, before saying, "I love you, Shay." She hung up before Shay could respond.

She couldn't remember the last time her mother said those words. She was left with a set of mixed emotions. She was sad over losing her father, angry with God for taking him away from her, and happy to hear her mother say something kind to her.

Chapter 16

Three days later

It was 2PM when Shay arrived on Janine's doorstep with Chloe and Caroline in tow. She knocked on the door, but despite Janine's car being in the driveway, there was no answer. Shay knocked a few more times, without a response, before digging the spare key out of her purse.

When they walked in, Shay saw her mother sitting on the living room floor with half a dozen photo albums spread in front of her.

"Mom?"

"Oh, Shay, um, you're here." Janine glanced at Chloe and smiled. "Hi, sweetheart."

Chloe walked to her and gave her a big hug. "Hi, Grandma."

Shay looked at Caroline. "Could you take Chloe outside for a bit? There are bubbles on the shelf in the garage."

"Sure."

Jason arrived just as they were heading to the yard. "Hey, Jason, come out with us," Caroline said to him.

Shay took a seat on the floor beside her mother. "What's that photo you're holding?"

Janine smiled. "This picture was taken two weeks after your father and I met in college. That was one of my best memories."

Shay wanted her mother to maintain that smile for as long as possible, so she asked a question that would extend her trip down memory lane. "You know, Mom, you and Dad never told me how you met. I'd love to hear the story."

"Oh, that night was like a classic scene out of a romance film. It was orientation day for the freshmen students. I was sitting next to my boyfriend at the time."

"Wait a second. You were in a relationship with another man when you met Dad? How scandalous," she teased.

Janine laughed a little. "His name was

Travis. He was my boyfriend since high school and a very sweet fellow, but I had doubts about where the relationship was headed. It wasn't until your father and I locked eyes from across the room, that I knew Travis and I weren't meant to be. I was too nervous to break it off. After all, I wasn't even sure if your father reciprocated the attraction."

"Who made the first move?"

"I excused myself to the bathroom as a pretext to initiate a conversation with him. We talked for a few minutes before he asked me on a date. After that, I knew what I had to do. So very gently, I let Travis down, and from thereafter, your father and I were inseparable."

"Wow, that is a really great story, Mom. Thank you for sharing it with me." She glanced at her watch. "Are you hungry? We have a little time before the wake."

"Why don't we order something? My treat."

"Who should we order from?"

"The Red Oak Diner, Arthur's favorite."

"Great idea. I bet Dad is looking down at us with mouth-watering envy."

About ten minutes after she placed the order, Janine drove to the diner. Everyone else took turns sharing stories about Shay's father. Once Janine came back, the reminiscing was put on hold while everyone dug into their food.

Once they finished eating, Janine drove everyone to the funeral parlor. Steve was already there, waiting for them. Leaving the others in a small room with couches and two Manhattan chairs, Shay, Steve, and Janine visited Arthur.

When they got up to the open casket, Shay studied her father, who was dressed in a light blue suit, complimented with a navy-blue tie and a gold watch banded with brown leather, given to him by Janine for their first anniversary.

"He looks so peaceful." Shay leaned her head against Steve's shoulder.

"And handsome," Janine sobbed through tears.

Steve wrapped his arms around them,

and after a few solemn minutes with Arthur, they took their seats in the front row. Then, right at that moment, several other friends and family members began to fill up the room.

A lot of the people who attended seemed to be at a loss for words, since most of the condolences fell within the traditional "I'm so sorry for your loss." So, by the middle of the viewing, Shay started to feel robotic with her responses. But that pattern was altered when Joe and Elaine Davis walked up with Corrine and Alyssa beside them.

Shay brightened when she saw her niece. "Hi, sweetie."

Alyssa walked closer and wrapped her arms around Shay's waist, then did the same to Steve. "I'm sorry about your daddy," she said to both of them.

Steve picked up Alyssa and gave her a kiss on the cheek. "Thank you, honey."

"I really loved your dad," Corrine said through tears. Her eyes shifted to Steve.

He placed Alyssa back on the floor. "I'm

really glad you guys are here."

Elaine said, "We were devastated when we heard about your dad." Her hands were shaking as she sympathetically touched Shay's hand.

"She's right," Joe chimed in. "Your dad was a great man, truly one in a million."

"Thank you. That means a lot to me."

Corrine's parents continued to list Arthur's many wonderful attributes until Janine made a sudden and not so subtle interruption. "We appreciate you coming, but with all due respect, you're holding up the line."

"Mom, they're just paying their respects," Shay said in their defense.

"And they have, so they can leave now and allow others to pay *their* respects."

"Your mom is right. We've overstayed our welcome." Elaine had extended Janine a high level of undeserved patience.

Shay gave each of them a hug. "Thank you for coming."

"Of course," Joe replied. Then he and Elaine went on their way with Corrine and

Alyssa walking behind them.

The viewing continued for fifteen minutes then everyone drove to St. Andrews Church for the funeral.

Once everyone was seated in the chapel, the ceremony began, and after a heartfelt sermon from the minister, Shay was called up to the pulpit to read her eulogy.

"I want to begin by thanking all of you for taking the time out of your busy schedules to honor the life of my dad, Arthur Collins. He was many things to all of us, a loyal friend, a caring husband, and a loving grandfather. To my brother and I, he was a treasured father. No matter how busy or tired he was, my dad always made time to be there for us. That was just who he was, a man of unconditional love and support for his family and his friends."

Shay got a little choked up. "My father was a person of unlimited loyalty and generosity toward all of the people in his life. There is nothing he wouldn't do for someone who needed his help. He would literally give you the shirt off his back, and one time he did. From that point forward, that homeless man was never cold again. I think we can all agree that my dad was unique in his ability to unfailingly love everyone and everything in his life, and for that he will forever be in our hearts. Thank you for always being there for us, Dad. We love you."

When Shay returned to her seat, Jason wrapped his arm around her, at which point she broke down, but as sad as she was about losing her dad, she was grateful to have Jason and Chloe.

Chapter 17

The next few months were unbearable. Arthur was the first thing Shay thought of when she woke up in the morning and the last thing she thought of before she went to bed. But she promised herself that his death would not be in vain. Shay had been making consistent efforts to repair her relationship with Janine. They spoke on the phone almost every day, but today was the first time they were seeing each other since Arthur's funeral.

Janine arrived on Shay's doorstep, carrying a big box of treats from their favorite bakery.

"Mom, you didn't have to bring anything." She took the box from Janine.

"It was my pleasure." Janine scanned the front room. "No Chloe today?"

"She's taking a nap."

"There's an Eminem cookie in there for

her when she wakes up."

"Thanks. Now, let's enjoy these sweets together."

"I'm glad we did this." Janine took a bite out of her chocolate croissant. She seemed nervous though. She kept tapping the floor with her foot and avoided eye contact with Shay.

"Is everything okay?"

"There's something I need to tell you, Shay, something I should have told you a long time ago. It's not something I could share with you over the phone."

"What is it?"

"It happened years before you were born. I was just starting out at the law firm, and I had this client whose case was complicated, to say the least. It was one of the only cases I'd ever lost, and he wasn't happy with me. I received threatening letters for almost a year. I think he just wanted to scare me, and it worked."

"Oh my God, Mom. I'm so sorry, but I'm a little confused. What does this have to do with me?"

"Honey, I was going through a very dark time in my life, and I had a hard time opening up to your dad about it. He was so busy with work and was too tired to talk when he got home. So, I found solace in a family friend."

"Okay?" *Where is she going with this?*

Janine took a deep breath. "We started talking, and then one thing led to another. I'm not proud of what I did, and after we slept together, we instantly regretted it. We promised to never speak a word of it to anyone."

Shay didn't understand how this concerned her, or why her mother felt the need to come clean about it now. Her father was gone, and Janine had already admitted that the affair was a mistake. "I can't say this revelation doesn't bother me, but it happened a long time ago, and everyone makes mistakes. What I don't get is why you're telling me."

"Because that's not the end of the story."

"Will you get to the point, Mom?"

"A few weeks after we slept together, I began to experience symptoms that made me think I was pregnant, so I took a test."

"Pregnant?" Shay's patience was decreasing rapidly. "Mom, what are you getting at?"

"Shay, this isn't easy for me to say, especially because of how much you loved Arthur and how much I know he loved you."

Had Janine gotten an abortion? Did Shay have another sibling? She didn't know what to think.

"Mom, just tell me."

"Shay, Arthur wasn't your father."

The color must've drained from Shay's face and she felt like she was going to throw up. "No, that's not true. Arthur is my father...always has been..." She kept choking on her words but forced them out anyway. "Always will be my dad."

"Shay, I'm so sorry," Janine sobbed out. "But it's true."

Gripping the edge of the table to help keep her steady in a room now spinning around her, she let her anger loose. "I can't believe you've lived another lie, Mom." Then came the flood of tears streaming down her face and a demand from her lips that erupted deep down in her throat as a growl. "Who is my real dad?"

"Joe Davis."

"Corrine's father?" she shouted.

"I know you're not happy to hear this, and understandably so, but please lower your voice."

"Let me get this straight." Shay brought her tone down a level by hissing through her clenched teeth. "For twenty-nine years, you hid the identity of my real father. You lied to me every day of my life. And to top it off, Corrine is my half-sister...we have the same father...and you kept that from me, as well. Are you the devil's spawn, or what?"

"Shay, I made a horrible mistake. I'm telling you now because I have really enjoyed these last few months with you, and I don't want there to be any more secrets or lies between us."

"You are unbelievable. Did dad know he wasn't my father?"

"He never said anything, but I think he had his suspicions."

"Why do you say that?"

"He asked me once if I was still happy with him. I said 'yes' and he immediately dropped the subject, but sometimes I would catch him staring at you, like he was studying your features and comparing them to his own."

"You should have come clean."

"I was scared. I didn't want to lose him."

"Clearly you didn't know him at all. He could have left you the minute he started having suspicions, but he didn't. He deserved better than your secrets."

"You're right."

"Does Joe know I'm his daughter?"

"He didn't at first, but a few years after you were born, he began to see a resemblance. I had to tell him the truth, and I made him promise not to say a word. The scandal would ruin both families."

"I can't believe you slept with your husband's best friend. Dad loved him like a brother. He had so much respect for Joe, so did I, for that matter. And now, I find out he's no better than the ice-cold woman sitting across from me."

"Shay, you have every right to hate me, but please don't blame Joe. He wanted to tell you."

"I can't listen to you anymore." Shay started to get up from the table, but her mother grabbed her hand.

"We can get through this, Shay."

"Let go of my hand and go back to California. I never want to see you again."

"Shay, you don't mean that."

"You are a despicable human being, and I do *not* want your influence around my kid. You and me, we're done."

Shay banged her head against the door. She knew she did the right thing, but it was still painful. They were making progress in their relationship, and now they didn't even have one.

Chapter 18

Jason was in New York to celebrate their four-month anniversary. The day started with breakfast, and then they took Chloe to see the Lion King on Broadway. Afterwards, Jason bought tickets to Luna Park, where they spent the afternoon enjoying the rides and pigging out on junk food. As they were walking off their corn dogs and cotton candy, Jason said, "Hey, babe, there's something I want to talk to you about."

Her stomach tightened. "What is it?"

"These last few months have been great. I'm falling more in love with you every day."

Shay smiled. "I like where this is going."

"I think we should move in together."

"Here in New York?"

"Yeah."

"What about your art gallery?"

"I have someone interested in buying it.

I said no at the time, but she gave me her card in case I changed my mind. So... what do you think?"

Shay was suddenly at a loss for words, so instead, she pulled him to a stop, turned him around to face her, and gave him a kiss.

"I'll take that as a yes."

Shay smiled and nodded.

When they got back to the apartment, there was a note from Caroline on the fridge: *Going out for a while. Be back late. Enjoy.* Shay smiled. The alone-time with Jason made her love Caroline even more.

Shay grabbed a few games from the hall closet and set them on the table. She and Jason killed some time before dinner by playing Candy Land and Go Fish with Chloe.

Later that night, after Chloe had gone to bed, Shay grabbed a couple of wine glasses from the cupboard and poured them each a glass of Chardonnay. She handed Jason his glass and held hers close for a toast. "To us."

"To us."

They took a few sips before Shay

grabbed both glasses and placed them on the coffee table. She straddled him on the couch and began to kiss him.

He pulled away and gazed into her eyes as if he'd found heaven there. "I love you."

"I love you too." She took his hand and led him to the bedroom where they celebrated the latest step in their relationship.

Chapter 19

Shay was enjoying her weekly Saturday night movie marathon with Caroline when Steve called. "Hey, Steve. How are you?"

"Corrine and I are back together." She heard enthusiasm in his voice.

"That's great news. I'm so happy for you guys."

"Thanks, Shay. That means a lot to me."

"Have you heard from Sherry?"

Steve laughed. "She reached out to me a few weeks after I called off the wedding and apologized."

"Wow. I'm surprised."

"I accepted her apology. I don't want to be angry anymore."

"Good for you, Steve. I have some news of my own. Jason and I are moving in together...here in New York."

"You two make a great couple."

"Thanks. I have to let you go now. Caroline and I are watching a movie."

"Okay, and have a happy birthday tomorrow."

Shay hung up. She had completely forgotten her birthday. Between juggling her job and taking care of Chloe, not to mention her long distance relationship with Jason, her birthday was the last thing on her mind. Tomorrow she'd say goodbye to her twenties and hello to her thirties, which promised to be a whole new world with Jason in her life.

***

The next morning, Shay woke up to the sound of Chloe bursting into the bedroom. "Happy birthday, Mommy." She plopped onto the bed and snuggled up next to her.

"Aww, thank you, sweetheart. I love you so much."

"Come on, Mommy." Chloe tugged on Shay's hand. "Auntie Caroline made breakfast."

When she entered the kitchen, she saw

a huge feast spread across the table. Caroline really went all out with bacon and eggs along with chocolate chip pancakes and a big bowl of fruit salad.

"Caroline, this looks amazing." She selected a plate from the cupboard.

"I couldn't let my best friend starve on her birthday. Hurry up and eat. We have a long day of shopping ahead of us."

Shay smiled. Every year, since their junior year in high school, she and Caroline would always go on a huge shopping spree for their birthdays. The tradition started after Caroline's ex-boyfriend broke up with her via text message the night before her birthday.

"What stores do we hit today?" Shay asked as she wolfed down her breakfast.

"Where do you feel like going?"

"Let's hit Times Square and take it from there."

"Sounds good to me."

***

While the three of them popped in and

out of various stores, Shay and Caroline enjoyed some girl talk.

"I have some fun news," Caroline said.

"Do tell."

"I've been talking to this guy I met online, and last week we finally decided to meet up."

"Why didn't you tell me sooner?"

"I didn't want to jinx it."

"Who is he?"

"His name is Jake. He works for an accounting firm. He's really nice and he's cute too."

"Always a plus. When are you going to meet him?"

"Next Saturday. He's taking me to dinner and a show. Speaking of next weekend, Sunday's the big move. It's a big step for you and Jason. Are you nervous at all?"

"Mostly excited. I think it's gonna be good for us."

"I'm really happy for you, Shay. You deserve it, which is why I thought you would enjoy this." Caroline reached in her purse and pulled out a gift certificate to Victoria's Secret. "Go have fun. Chloe and I will meet you back at the apartment."

"Aww, Caroline, thank you so much."

Inside Victoria's Secret, Shay browsed the entire store twice before finding the perfect lingerie, a pink satin cross-back slip with black lace around the cleavage, along with a matching satin robe. She knew Jason would love it on her and even more-so taking it off her.

When she returned to the apartment, Caroline was sprawled out on their couch, sipping from a big glass of soda. "Hey, birthday girl. Have fun?"

"I found the perfect teddy to wear next Sunday night."

"I ordered pizza a few minutes ago, so it should be here in a bit."

"Cool."

While they were waiting for their food, Shay got a call from Jason.

"Happy birthday, Shay."

"Thanks, honey. It's been a great day. I wish you could have been here with me."

"Have you gotten any other birthday calls, like maybe from Joe or your mom?"

"I talked to Steve last night, and Joe called me while I was shopping with Caroline and Chloe. As far as my mom is concerned, she called but I didn't answer. The truth is, I don't know when or if we'll ever be on talking terms again."

She and Jason talked a little longer until the pizza arrived. Then she, Caroline, and Chloe spent the rest of the evening watching movies. It was the best way to end a great birthday.

Chapter 20

Matt's visit

Shay sat at her kitchen table, nervously drinking her coffee before Matt came by for his visit with Chloe. She wanted to tell him about her and Jason but wasn't sure how he would take the news. Matt never liked him.

He arrived on time. "I can't believe I get to see Chloe without a social worker."

Shay smiled. "You've earned it, Matt. I'm so proud of you."

"Thanks."

Chloe ran out of her room and right into Matt's arms. "Daddy," she said, with a big smile and wrapped her arms around him.

"Hey, buttercup, I missed you."

"Can we go to the park now?" Chloe grabbed his hand and started for the door.

"One second, buttercup." He looked back at Shay. "I've been doing a lot of thinking. I know I wasn't a good husband to you, but I want to be the best father I can be for Chloe. The only way I can do that, is to move here. I went online and began looking for apartments in New York."

"Matt, that's great, really, but there's something you should know before you move here."

"What's that?"

"Jason and I are a couple now, and he's moving here so we can live together."

Matt smiled. "Shay, don't worry. Jason and you moving in together isn't going to make me start drinking again."

"I just wanted to give you a heads up. I know how you feel about him."

"If he makes you happy and he's good to Chloe, then he's okay in my book."

"Daddy, let's go," Chloe said with impatience.

Matt laughed. "Bye, Shay."

Chloe ran back quickly to give Shay a hug. "Bye, Mommy."

"Bye, sweetie. Have fun with your dad."

After they left, she took out her laptop

and began looking over the latest manuscript assigned to her. After two hours of editing, she was ready to take a break. Matt's visit was just about over, giving her an excuse to walk away from her computer.

Matt arrived with Chloe just as Shay entered the living room.

"I'll see you again soon, sweetie." Matt hugged Chloe goodbye.

"Okay, Daddy. I love you."

"I love you too, buttercup." He headed for the door.

"Wait, Matt. Why don't you stay a little longer? I'll make us lunch."

"That'd be great."

"Daddy, come with me, I want to show you what I made at school." Chloe grabbed his hand and led him to the hallway, where Shay had hung a few of her drawings on the wall.

"Wow, Chloe, these should be hanging in an art museum."

Shay smiled. This was the Matt she knew, sober, reliable, and a loving dad.

Chapter 21

Shay spent the rest of the week in a daze. Since Jason's move was approaching, it was difficult to focus on anything else. So naturally, when his moving day finally came, she wasted no time in preparing for his arrival.

She thought the best way to prep was to give herself a spa treatment, but to save the cost of going to a professional, she and Caroline enjoyed a do-it-yourself spa day.

They sat Chloe in the living room with them, and as she played with her doll, they took turns giving one another mani-pedis. Usually, Shay chose sky blue for her fingernails and navy-blue for her toes, but since this was a special occasion, she opted for a sultry red and passion pink combo.

While Caroline was painting Shay's toenails, she looked up. "I have news." She took a deep breath. "I've decided it's time for me to move out."

"Move out?" Shay felt blindsided. "Why? There's enough room here for the four of us."

Caroline smiled at her. "You and Jason are starting a new chapter in your lives, and my room may come in handy one day." She winked.

Shay knew, in her heart, that Caroline made sense, but that didn't ease her disappointment. "Where will you go?"

"My mom's...until I find my own place."

"Okay, as long as you know that this wasn't my idea. I love having you as a roommate, and I would never ask you to leave."

"I know that, silly. It's entirely my decision."

"Good."

Once their nails were painted and dried, Shay and Caroline got up, ready to head into the kitchen to make mud masks for themselves, along with a cucumber eye gel. They didn't want to exclude Chloe, so Shay gave her plain cucumber slices to put over her eyes and when their facials were completed, both Shay and Caroline gave a sigh of deep satisfaction. Never in their lives had they felt so relaxed.

Even Chloe chimed in. "Mommy, I feel like a new woman."

Shay and Caroline burst out with uncontrollable laughter. She was truly the most adorable child in the world.

When Shay looked at the clock and saw the time, she switched from stress-free to panic-stricken. "Jason's going to be here in less than two hours. I'm not even close to being ready."

"Relax, Shay. I'll help you pick out the perfect outfit, shoes and all. Then Chloe and I will get dressed and head over to my mom's house."

Shay gave Caroline a huge hug. "Thank you so much. You're truly the best friend a girl can ask for."

"You'll owe me big time."

With that said, the two of them flew into Shay's bedroom and rifled through her closet. After trying on three dresses three times, they finally came to a decision: a black sleeveless dress, medium length, with a deep neckline and a beautiful pattern of straps in the back. Top that off with two-inch heels, and Shay had the perfect combination of classy and sexy.

"Okay, now that you have your outfit picked out, I'm going to get dressed and pack overnight bags for Chloe and myself."

As soon as the door shut, Shay quickly but carefully put her dress on and strapped on her heels. Then she walked out of her room and into the bathroom to grab her makeup bag. As she was applying her black eyeliner, Chloe called for her.

"Mommy, I wanna stay here with you." She stood in the doorway and showed Shay her sad puppy-dog eyes.

Normally, that look broke Shay's resolve, but this time she stayed strong. "Aw, sweetie, you're going to have so much fun with auntie Caroline and her mom. You won't even notice I'm not there."

"I want to see Jason too."

Caroline stepped up behind her. "It's

only one night, Chloe." She took Chloe's hand. "You'll be back tomorrow morning. I promise you will see him then."

"Okay. Bye, Mommy."

"Bye, sweetie. Mommy loves you so much." Shay gave her a kiss on the cheek and a big squeeze. "I'll see you guys tomorrow."

Once they were gone, Shay finished applying her eyeliner, followed by a light brown eyeshadow and a dark red lipstick to complement her dress.

When she was finished, she ran a brush through her hair, then proceeded to the living room, where she only had to wait ten minutes before Jason knocked on the door.

With his black leather jacket, navy-blue button-down shirt, and black slacks, it was as if they had color-coordinated their outfits. As soon as she saw him, she wrapped her arms around his neck and gave him a big kiss.

"Now that's the way a guy likes to be greeted," Jason said, as he pulled away to hand her a crystal vase filled with a dozen pink tulips. "Happy belated birthday, beautiful."

"Aww, Jason, thank you." She walked into the kitchen and placed the vase on the table.

"You're welcome. I'm just sorry I wasn't able to give them to you on your actual birthday."

"This is the next best thing. Should we look online for a good place to eat?"

"I made reservations at Carmine's."

"That sounds great. It was the first Italian restaurant I went to when I moved here."

"I know. I called Caroline last week and asked her what restaurants you liked."

"Aww, Jason, that was so sweet." She gave him another kiss then grabbed her jacket and purse.

Jason led Shay to his rental car and opened her door.

It was a good thing they had reservations, since there was a huge line of people waiting when they arrived. They took a few minutes to peruse the menu, and after scrolling through the entrees a couple of times, they finally decided on the Veal Parmigiana for Shay and the Penne Ala Vodka for Jason. Then once they placed their orders with the waitress, they began to talk about the past two months they'd spent apart.

"How did it go with selling your house?" Shay asked.

"The house was in good condition, so I was able to get a good price for it."

They talked a little longer, before their food came. After they finished eating, Jason paid the bill, and they hustled back to his car. For the first time since Jason received his license, he drove ten miles an hour over the speed limit. As soon as they got back to the apartment, Shay hung up their jackets, and then she took Jason's hand and started to lead him to the bedroom.

"Wait." He gently pulled her back.

"What's wrong?"

"There's just something I want to say before we do anything."

Shay's heart began to race. "Okay, what

is it?"

"Shay, you have always been my best friend. I can tell you things that I've never felt comfortable telling anyone else. You're the complete package, beautiful, warm, and the strongest person I have ever met. What I love most though, is that you never waiver in your ability to show compassion and loyalty to those around you. I want to spend the rest of my life waking up next to you."

He reached into his coat pocket and pulled out a ring box. Then he got down on one knee and opened the box to reveal a stunning white gold Marquise Diamond engagement ring. "This belonged to my mom. A few years ago, my aunt gave it to me and made me promise her that I would hold onto it until I found the right woman. I can't think of a more perfect person to wear it. Shay Collins, will you marry me?"

She smiled. "Yes." She threw her arms around his neck and kissed his lips. Then he stood up and carried her into the bedroom where they spent the next hour celebrating their engagement.

Chapter 22

Shay woke up the next morning and stared at her engagement ring. It was more beautiful than she could have ever imagined. A part of her was still in shock and disbelief. She'd spent most of her life secretly in love with this man and fantasized about a life with him, but never in her wildest dreams did she think a marriage would happen. After a few minutes of taking in the beauty of her diamond, she turned to embrace her fiancé.

"Morning, beautiful," he muttered. "How'd you sleep?"

"I didn't sleep much. My adrenaline kept me up most of the night."

Jason chuckled. "Let me guess, you already started planning our wedding."

"You know me so well."

"I have an idea for the date."

"What date do you have in mind?"

"August 12th. Arthur's birthday."

She teared up a bit. "I love that idea. It will be like he's there with us."

"That's good for a start." He smiled.

The front door squeaked open, and Shay heard Chloe call for her. She and Jason scrambled to put on clothes and opened the bedroom door just as Chloe was about to burst in.

"Mommy." She jumped into Shay's arms.

"Hi, sweetie." Shay gave her a kiss. "Did you and auntie Caroline have a good time with her mom?"

"We made s'mores and watched *two* movies."

"Did you stay up late?"

"Caroline said it was okay."

"I'm glad you had fun, sweetie." She set Chloe's feet on the floor.

"Jason," she squealed and embraced his leg.

"Hi, Chloe." He knelt to give her a hug. "Thanks for letting me spend some alone-time with your mom last night."

"You're welcome." She ran to her

bedroom to play with her toys.

Jason looped his arm around Shay. "I'm gonna stay in here for a bit and start unpacking my things while you girls talk."

"Thanks, honey." She pointed to the dresser. "I cleared a couple of drawers for you last week and organized the closet, so you'll have plenty of space."

In the living room, Caroline looked curiously at Shay. "How did it go last night?"

Shay lifted her hand to show Caroline her engagement ring. "He asked me to marry him."

Caroline's eyes beamed with delight. "I am so happy for you guys."

"I'd love for you to be my Maid of Honor."

"Of course."

After a few giddy moments, Shay walked into Chloe's room to tell her the good news. "Hey, sweetie, Mommy has something really exciting to tell you."

Chloe stopped playing with her toys. "What is it?"

"You like Jason, right?"

"Yeah, he's really nice."

Shay smiled and began to stroke Chloe's hair. "I'm glad, because last night Jason asked me to marry him."

"Does that mean he's my new daddy?" Chloe frowned. She looked confused.

"No, honey. You will always have the same daddy. Jason is just going to be a new member of our family."

"Oh. Cool." Chloe broke away from Shay and went back to her toys.

After leaving Chloe's room, Shay grabbed her phone to call Steve with her good news.

"Congratulations, sis."

"I'm so excited."

"Have you told anyone else?"

"You mean Mom? No."

"Are you going to?"

Shay sighed. "A part of me wants to, but the other part is still so angry and hurt. I don't know how to forgive her."

"What about Joe?"

"We've talked a few times over the phone. I haven't completely forgiven him but I'm getting there."

"I get it. It took a while for me to get over what Mom did to me and Corrine."

"How did you do it?"

"I realized forgiveness isn't just for the person who needs to be forgiven. I've been a lot happier since I reached out to Mom."

"I hate it when you're right."

Steve chuckled. "It's a blessing and a curse."

After her call with Steve, she held her phone close to her chest and took a deep breath, and then called her mother.

"Shay? Hi. I, um, I'm surprised to hear from you."

"I have some big news and thought I should share it with you. Jason and I are engaged."

"Oh, Shay, that's wonderful."

"Thank you."

"Shay, I know what I did was awful, but if you would allow me to, I'd really love to come to your wedding."

"I'd like that too."

"You probably want to spend time with

Jason and Chloe now. Thanks for the call."

Steve was right. Shay hadn't realized how much she missed her mom until she heard her voice. Maybe a relationship between them was still possible.

When she got off the phone with Janine, she walked into the living room to find Caroline sitting on the couch with several bridal magazines spread out in front of her. "Where did you get all of these?"

"I've accumulated them over the years." Caroline grinned. "I kept them in a box under my bed, just in case someone ever wants to marry me."

She sat next to Caroline, and they perused the magazines like a couple of giddy teenagers.

"Let's start with dresses," Caroline said. "What style were you thinking to wear?"

"I'm a simple girl. You remember the dress I wore for my wedding with Matt, a basic floor-length V-neck?"

"Jason is not Matt. We are *not* looking for something basic. We need to find you something exquisite."

"How much is it going to cost me?"

They looked through magazine after magazine and found various dress styles that Shay admired, but none of them stood out as being *the perfect dress*. They set the dress search on the back burner and moved onto venues, and the more time Shay spent browsing, the more she realized that getting married wasn't easy.

Chapter 23
The Wedding

After she spent months making phone calls and meeting with various vendors, Shay was finally standing in the Ritz-Carlton bridal suite in New York, waiting to become Mrs. Jason Kent.

She was too excited and anxious to sit with her bridal party: Caroline, Corrine, Chloe, and Alyssa, so instead, she stood in front of the full-length mirror and gazed at her dream dress. It was a stunning sleeveless ballgown with a deep V-neckline and beautiful lace detail around the straps and keyhole back. It had taken her a while to find it, but once she laid her eyes on the dress, she knew she was meant to wear it.

"You look like a princess, Mommy," Chloe said.

"Aww, thank you, sweetie, but I don't look half as amazing as my flower girl and junior bridesmaid." Shay winked at Alyssa and Chloe.

"You are absolutely gorgeous," Corrine said.

"I owe it all to my Maid of Honor. Caroline must have taken me to fifteen bridal stores before we made any decisions. She refused to let me settle for anything less than flawless."

Corrine smiled at Caroline. "Good job, girl. She looks flawless."

Caroline took a bow.

There was a knock at the door. "It's just me." Janine walked in. "Oh, honey, you look gorgeous."

"Thanks, Mom."

"I wanted to give this to you before you walk down the aisle." She handed Shay a gold heart-shaped locket with a floral pattern around the edges. Inside, was a picture of Shay and Arthur.

"Good thing I'm wearing waterproof eyeliner." Shay hugged her mother tight. "Thank you. I miss him so much."

"I do too." Janine pulled away gently. "I

should go take my seat now. See you soon."

After Janine left, Shay stood proudly with her girls, thinking of how perfect her wedding would be. Her only other wish was that Arthur was still alive to walk her down the aisle.

Three raps sounded on the door, the signal to come out of the room.

Shay smiled, beaming with joy. "This is it." She took a deep breath.

The bridal party walked one-by-one into the hotel ballroom while Shay stood next to her brother, brimming with eager anticipation. The Bridal March emanated from the sound system, signaling the bride to make her entrance. Steve looped arms with her, and as they proceeded down the aisle, he whispered, "Dad would be so proud."

Shay had to choke back her tears.

As they continued down the aisle, Shay could feel everyone's eyes on her. She glanced at her mother, who, to her surprise, was sitting next to Joe and Elaine. She caught them whispering to one another and smiling. She exchanged a few smiles with her other friends and family members, but the primary focus of her vision was on Jason. He looked so handsome, wearing his black tuxedo with a slick lapel and black bowtie.

Shay was steps away from her groom, feeling excited and eager, but also a little nervous. The last time she'd walked down the aisle, she thought the marriage would last forever, until it didn't. She was a firm believer, though, that everything happened for a reason. That reason had to be Jason, the first man she'd fallen in love with.

When they reached the front of the room, Steve kissed her hand and joined it with Jason's. He then took a seat in the front row, and the Justice of the Peace began the ceremony.

She spoke a few words on the value of love and the rarity of finding a soulmate. Then she handed the ceremony over to Shay and Jason for the sharing of their vows.

"Shay, I have always known you to be kind, compassionate, loyal, and incredibly strong. You have always been my rock; someone I could confide in and trust. Today, I vow to show you that same kindness and compassion, for as long as we both live. I love you more than you could possibly know, and I always will."

"Jason, I have spent a good portion of my life being in love with you. Your warmth, generosity, and dedication to those around you, are just a few of the reasons why I adore you. I vow to spend the rest of my life showing you how much you mean to me."

The Justice of the Peace had them exchange rings and said those long-awaited words. "Shay, do you take Jason to be your lawfully wedded husband?"

"I do."

"And Jason, do you take Shay to be your lawfully wedded wife?"

"I do."

"By the power vested in me by the state of New York, I now pronounce you man and wife." She looked to Jason. "You may kiss your bride."

Jason cupped Shay's face with both hands and brought her in for a gentle kiss. Then they walked down the aisle, hand-in-hand, with everyone applauding behind them. Once they were out the door, she felt an overwhelming sense of accomplishment wash over her. She had an amazing daughter, wonderful friends, and a family she loved, and now she had Jason, the last piece of her life's puzzle.

Chapter 24

After spending a beautiful week-long honeymoon in Hawaii, Shay and Jason returned home. They ate a nice dinner, then spent the rest of the evening hanging out with Caroline and Chloe.

Shortly after Caroline left, Shay and Jason tucked Chloe into bed, and since they were exhausted from their long flight home, they followed suit. Shay found herself tossing and turning most of the night. Then at around 6AM, she started to feel nauseous, took an Alka-Seltzer, then Pepto-Bismol, but nothing in the medicine cabinet seemed to be helping. She'd been feeling nauseous for the past few days but wrote it off as a stomach bug. Maybe it wasn't though. She headed to the pharmacy for a pregnancy tester.

As soon as she came back, Shay raced

to the bathroom to vomit again, then proceeded to take the test. A few minutes later, she opened the door and found Jason waiting for her in the hallway. "Everything okay?"

"I'm more than okay." Shay handed Jason a pregnancy test with a neon blinking plus sign.

"Oh my God." Jason wrapped his arms around her. "I'm going to be a dad. This calls for a celebration."

He walked into the kitchen and grabbed the ingredients to make all of Shay's favorite breakfast foods, chocolate chip pancakes being at the top of the menu. Then after they finished eating, he started cleaning up. "I got this. Go relax."

"You're such a good husband." She walked into the living room with Chloe.

Jason joined them a few minutes later with Shay's phone in his hand. "I thought you'd want to make a few calls."

She took the phone from him. "Thank you."

"Who are you going to call first?"

Shay smiled. "My mom."

Janine screamed into the phone when Shay told her the news. "I'm so excited for you." She started to cry a little. "I'm going to be a grandma again."

"Thanks, Mom."

"I have vacation time coming up. I can fly down and help you with whatever you need."

"I'd love that, thank you."

After Shay got off the phone with her mom, she retreated to the kitchen where she made a few more calls, and then she walked back into the living room to cuddle up next to Jason.

He was truly the epitome of a perfect husband, and she knew without a doubt that he would be nothing less than a perfect father to their son or daughter.

Chapter 25

Shay loved how excited Jason was to be a father. Throughout her pregnancy, he had been nothing short of loving and attentive. From the moment she told him she was pregnant, he doted on her, whether that meant rubbing her feet, massaging her back, or running to the store at 12AM to satisfy a food craving.

However, he wasn't the only one providing her queen treatment. Caroline came to the apartment once a week with different necessities for Shay, which included chocolates, gossip magazines, and a home-spa kit. She also threw a beautiful baby shower for her, with help from Corrine and Janine, who flew in from California.

Though, as much as Shay enjoyed being pampered, there was a part of her that desired a little space, specifically from Jason. As sweet and wonderful as he was to her, he worried a lot and had the tendency to hover over her. Today was no different.

"Good morning, beautiful." He rubbed her pregnant belly.

"Good morning." She slowly twisted her body to get out of bed.

"What are you doing?"

Shay frowned at him. "I need to make breakfast for Chloe before we leave on our mommy-daughter day, remember?"

"Shay, you're eight and a half months pregnant. I know you want to spend alone-time with Chloe, but you can do that here."

She smiled sweetly at her husband, while slightly giggling. "Honey, I know you're worried, but I can still do everyday tasks as long as I'm careful. Plus, we're only going to the park and then lunch later."

"Okay," Jason said reluctantly.

When Shay walked into the living room, Chloe was sitting on the couch, watching her Saturday morning cartoons. She gave her a kiss on the head, then walked into the kitchen to prepare their breakfast of cereal and toast. After they finished eating, Shay got Chloe ready for the park. They played catch for a while and swung on the swings, too. Then Shay took a seat on the park bench while Chloe played in the sandbox.

By the time lunch rolled around, Shay was exhausted. She took Chloe to McDonalds before heading back home. When they walked in, Jason was at the kitchen table, finishing his lunch, but Shay was too tired to walk that far. The living room couch was closer.

"How was the park?" He walked in to give her a kiss.

"Chloe wore me out. I need a nap." She stood from the couch and waved Chloe to join her. "You should take a nap too, honey."

"I don't want to," Chloe whined.

"Just try."

Chloe's lower lip turned down. "Fine." She stomped to her bedroom in protest.

Shay shuffled after her, but Jason stopped her. "I have a surprise for you."

"I'm really tired, honey."

"Humor me."

She sat back down on the couch and

wondered what her husband was up to. Only then did she notice he was holding something behind his back.

"Close your eyes and put out your hands."

Shay held out her hands and felt something big and flat placed in her upturned palms.

"Open," Jason sang.

"Oh, my Goodness." Shay stared at a portrait of Arthur and her, taken when she was a little girl.

She remembered seeing this picture a hundred times over the years. Arthur was kneeling next to her in the living room, in front of the bookcase, both all smiles and staring at the camera. She was wearing a powder blue sundress and white sandals decorated with sunflowers.

"Do you like it?"

"I love it. When did you do this?"

"A couple of weeks after you told me you were pregnant. I emailed your mom and asked her to send me a few pictures of you and Arthur from when you were a kid.

She sent me a bunch, but I thought this one was perfect."

"Oh, honey, thank you so much. It's amazing."

"I'm so glad you like it." Jason gave her a kiss then helped her up from the couch. "Now go get some rest."

Shay entered the bedroom, immediately snuggled under her blanket, and fell into a deep sleep. When she woke up, it was almost 3PM and she felt a familiar craving.

"Jason?" She got up and waddled into the living room.

"What's your desire, madam?"

"Now you can read my mind?"

"I know the look."

"We're in the mood for tacos." She patted her stomach.

"Sure thing. Chloe just woke up. I'll take her with me to get them."

"Thank you so much, baby. You're the best husband ever."

"That's what I'm here for." He grabbed his car keys off the counter. "We'll be back."

Once they were out the door, Shay went

back into the bedroom and turned on the TV. Fifteen minutes into her show, her stomach started to rumble, loud and with force. She didn't know how close Jason and Chloe were, but she needed something to eat right now. Peanut butter bread, a jelly roll, pickles: anything.

As she rushed into the kitchen, she stepped on one of Chloe's toys, a doll by the way it cried out, and the room suddenly tilted. Her arms wind-milled as she tried to keep from falling, but her knees buckled, and she hit her head on the counter before she face-planted the floor.

Unfortunately, her baby bump took the first impact.

Oh, God, no. What have I done?

She couldn't get her feet up under her to stand, and blood was running into her eyes, blurring her vision, but she was able to extend her arm up to reach the strap of her purse resting on the table. She pulled it down and frantically searched for her phone, until it was finally in her grasp. She called 911 then prayed for her baby's safety.

While she lay there, waiting for help to arrive, she forced herself to keep her eyes open, but she was losing blood from a gash in her forehead, and her brain was feeling woozier by the second.

Please, God, let us be okay.

She felt a hand on her shoulder.

"Thank God you're here, Jason."

"Stay with me, Shay. The ambulance is almost here."

Shay felt her body getting weaker. "I can't."

"Yes, you can. You're stronger than you know, Shay. Just keep your eyes open a few more minutes."

She felt her eyes roll back in their sockets.

His face was just a blur, then nothing.

The next thing she knew, she was lying in a bed. White walls. White ceiling. Beeping machines.

A hospital. I'm in a hospital? A shot of adrenaline seared through her veins. She tried to sit up, but her body wouldn't obey.

Jason sprang to her side. "Shay. Take it

easy."

"What happened?"

"You took a bad fall."

"I fell?" She rubbed her head, discovered it wrapped in bandages.

"What do you remember?"

"I went to the kitchen for something to eat, ended up on the floor. You put your hand on my shoulder, then everything went blank."

Jason gave her a confused look. "What are you talking about, honey? I wasn't there."

"Of course you were. All I remember is a blurry face, but I think it was you by my side."

"It wasn't me. Chloe and I were still out getting tacos. When I got home, the ambulance was pulling away and cops had a million questions. You must have been hallucinating."

"I know I saw someone, Jason." She reached down to rub her pregnant belly, but something was wrong. The baby was gone. Panic threatened to steal her breath. "Oh,

God, no. What happened to our baby?" She started to cry, fearing the worst.

Jason let out a deep sigh. "The force of your fall caused a placental abruption." His eyes teared. "The doctors decided a cesarean was the safest bet for his survival. He's in the NICU, in an incubator. The doctors are taking good care of him."

"It's a boy?" She smiled through her tears.

"Our son, yes."

"Jason, what if they can't help him? What if I never get to hold my baby?" She started to hyperventilate.

Jason stroked her hair. "We can't think that way. Instead, let's decide on a name for him." He reached into his pocket and pulled out the list of baby names they'd compiled during her pregnancy.

Shay smiled and pointed to the first name on the boys' side of the list. "Let's call him Arthur."

"Arthur Kent. I love it."

She lifted her head to look around the room. "Where's Chloe?"

"I dropped her off with Caroline on my way to the hospital. I can bring her to visit in the morning. In the meantime, you should get some rest. You've had a long day."

She frowned. "It's hard to relax. I'm so worried about our son."

Jason kissed her forehead. "I know, but all you can do for him now is get your strength back."

"You're right." She reached for the remote and flipped through the channels until she found a funny sitcom to take her mind off the day's trauma. Then she closed her eyes and listened to the laughter of the audience, until she finally fell into a deep sleep.

Chapter 26

It was 9:00 the next morning when Shay woke up. Jason was sitting in the armchair across from her, and when he noticed her gaze, he slowly stood and walked to her bedside. "Good morning, beautiful. How'd you sleep?"

"Better than I have in weeks. I haven't felt this rested, in, I don't know how long."

Jason smiled. "I'm glad to hear that, because I thought we could visit our son."

Shay smiled wide. "Yes."

Jason wheeled her to the NICU. When they reached little Arthur's glass bassinet, she slowly rose from the wheelchair, using Jason's arm for support. She looked down at her beautiful baby, diapered and wearing a cute blue cap. His cheeks were chubby, and his pink lips twitched a little. An oxygen tube had been placed in his nose, just precautionary, as were the heart monitor wires attached to his chest. Shay teared up as she silently prayed that he wasn't injured in the fall.

She turned to Jason. "I want to hold him in the worst way."

He was teary-eyed and sniffled. "The doctors need to monitor him for a few days."

They stayed with the baby a little longer, then headed back to her room, where Chloe was waiting for her, with Caroline standing close by.

Chloe started to run to Shay, but Jason slowed her down. "Just be careful, honey."

Chloe gave her a cautious hug.

"Hey, Shay. How's it going?"

"I'm feeling better, Caroline, now that my favorite girl is here."

"How's the baby?"

"Little Arthur is a fighter."

"With that name, how could he not be?"

Shay looked at Chloe. "Would you like to meet your baby brother later?"

Chloe jammed her hands firmly on her hips and frowned. "No. I'm the baby around here."

Her blunt statement made the adults burst out laughing.

"Awe, sweetie, you will always be Mommy's baby, too."

Caroline reached into her pocket for her keys. "Come on, Chloe. Time to go."

"Thanks for watching her, Caroline." Shay hugged them goodbye. "And you, my little honeybee, Mommy loves you so much. I'll be home before you know it."

After Caroline left with Chloe, Steve walked in with Corrine and Alyssa.

The room suddenly felt more like home. "Hey, this is such a nice surprise. I wasn't expecting you guys to come."

Steve strode to her bedside and gave her a hug, then he turned to look around the room. "Where's my nephew?"

"In the NICU."

Corrine squeezed herself between them. "We'll be holding that kid in no time." She winked at Shay.

"Hey, honey," Jason said. "I'm a little hungry. I'm going to head downstairs to the cafeteria. Do you want me to bring you back anything?"

"No. I'm okay."

"I'll be back in a few." Jason bent down to give her a kiss.

When he left, Shay looked at Alyssa. "Hey, sweetie. Can I have a hug?"

Alyssa climbed onto the bed and carefully wrapped her arms around Shay. "I love you, auntie Shay."

"I love you too."

Corrine picked up Alyssa and handed her to Steve. "So how are you and your mom doing?"

"We're okay. As angry as I was with her for what she did, I gained an awesome sister." Shay held her arms out for a hug.

"I know what you mean." Corrine returned the embrace. "Oh, before I forget, my parents wanted me to give this to you." She handed Shay a baby-themed gift bag.

Shay was touched when she looked inside and pulled out a hand-knitted blue and green baby blanket along with a matching cap and booties.

"Oh my God, your mom made these? They're so beautiful."

"It was a team effort. My mom made the blanket, Dad made the cap, and I made the booties."

"Wow, I didn't realize Joe knew how to knit."

"He didn't until recently. He asked my mom to teach him. You should have heard the swearing that day." Corrine clapped a hand over her mouth to control her laughter.

"Please tell them I said thank you, and that I love everything."

"I will." Corrine turned to Steve and smiled. "Are you going to say something?"

"What's going on?" Shay asked.

"We weren't sure if today was the right day to share this with you, but I think there's always room for good news." He and Corrine looked at each other for a moment before turning their heads back to Shay. "Last night I asked Corrine to marry me, and she said yes."

"My God, Steve. It's about time."

"Awesome," Jason chimed in as he

walked through the door.

"We couldn't be happier." Steve gathered Corrine and Alyssa close to him.

The wedding talk continued for another ten minutes before Steve decided to let Shay have some time alone with Jason. However, once they left, Shay found it hard to keep her eyes open, so Jason encouraged her to take a nap.

She slept for a few hours but when she woke up, she was feeling restless. She'd been stuck in the hospital room for hours on end. The only time she rose from her bed was when she felt the urge to use the bathroom, and when she visited Arthur, she was in a wheelchair most of the time. So when one of her nurses, Becky, walked in and asked if she'd like to take a trip down the hall, she nodded with enthusiasm.

"You have two choices. I can grab a wheelchair for you, or you can walk on your own, as long as Jason is beside you."

"I can walk."

"Okay then. I'll leave you to it."

After Nurse Becky left, Jason slowly

helped her out of bed, and they carefully walked out of the room.

"I bet it feels pretty good to finally be up and walking, huh."

"You have no idea."

They got halfway down the hall, before she started to feel tired.

"I don't think I can make it all the way down the hall, hon. I better get back to bed."

"No problem." He helped her turn around.

When they got back to the room, he helped her back in the bed and offered her a cup of water. As she sipped her water, the fuzziness of the night Arthur was born suddenly became clear:

As she struggled to stay awake, she could feel the energy leaving her body. Then suddenly, she sensed a man standing over her. He leaned down to put his hand on her shoulder. "Stay with me, Shay, the ambulance is almost here," the voice said. "I can't." Shay was feeling weaker and weaker. "Yes, you can. You're stronger than you know, Shay. Just keep your eyes open a few more minutes." Those words gave her the encouragement she needed to stay awake until the paramedics rushed in. Just before she passed out, she saw the face of the man above her, if only for a second before her vision blurred and went black.

It was Arthur.

Shay had heard of experiences like this, but she never thought it could happen, until now. Shay smiled inwardly. She realized that, while her father was no longer around, she could still count on him to be there for her when it really mattered.

A swarm of thoughts buzzed in her head as she lay in bed. She thought of how lucky she was, for her friends, her family, her husband, and her beautiful children. Then she lifted her head up slightly and hoped her father, wherever he was, could hear her now.

"I love you, Dad."

About the Author

Katelyn Marie Peterson graduated from Southern Connecticut State University with a bachelor's degree in journalism and writes freelance pieces for various newspapers. When she isn't typing on her laptop, she enjoys movie marathons, singing show tunes in the car, and cozying up with a good book. Katelyn resides in Connecticut with her husband and two children, a stay-at-home mom with a passion for writing Romance.

Made in United States
North Haven, CT
02 June 2022